# MURDER ON FLEET STREET

A COZY HISTORICAL 1920S MYSTERY

## LEE STRAUSS

Library and Archives Canada Cataloguing in Publication Title: Murder on Fleet Street : a cozy historical 1920s mystery / Lee Strauss. Names: Strauss, Lee (Novelist), author. Series: Strauss, Lee (Novelist). Ginger Gold mystery ; 12. Description: Series statement: A Ginger Gold mystery ; 12 Identifiers: Canadiana (print) 20190196807 | Canadiana (ebook) 20190196815 | ISBN 9781774090756 (softcover) | ISBN 9781774090763 (hardcover) | ISBN 9781774090770 (IngramSpark softcover) | ISBN 9781774090732 (EPUB) | ISBN 9781774090749 (Kindle) Classification: LCC PS8637.T739 M89 2019 | DDC C813/.6—dc23

## GINGER GOLD MYSTERIES

$\mathcal{M}$rs. Ginger Reed, also known around the city of London as Lady Gold, loved a good party. And if the official adoption of her son, Scout, wasn't a fabulous reason to celebrate, then she couldn't think of what was.

"Isn't it funny how things turn out?" she said as her husband Basil swept her around the drawing room and they swirled past large portraits which were set off to perfection by the ivory and green art deco wallpaper. A three-piece band had set up in the corner of the large drawing room at Hartigan House, Ginger's childhood home in South Kensington, and played the spirited notes of jazz.

"I couldn't be happier," Basil replied, smiling. His hazel eyes twinkled enough to make Ginger's heart burst with pride. She'd chosen her rose georgette gown with the sequinned, double-scalloped skirt especially because she knew it was one of his favourites. Her long strand of beads complemented the pearly-white bead trim in the hem, and a dramatic red bow was stitched low on the hipline. She'd pinned back her red bob, newly styled in finger waves that morning, with a delicate hair clip trimmed with rhinestones.

Dancing was a favourite pastime for Ginger and Basil. They'd met officially for the first time on the dance floor of a club on the SS *Rosa* during a steamship journey from Boston to Liverpool. It was also there where they'd met their son, Scout, who'd worked in the belly of the ship tending to the animals, including in the pet kennel where Ginger's Boston terrier, Boss, had spent time.

The ballroom at Hartigan House wasn't as large as those found in some houses, but with the furniture pushed back, it was plenty big enough for a crowd this size.

Felicia, Ginger's youthful former sister-in-law, also lived at Hartigan House. She danced with a rather attractive constable who worked under Basil in Basil's position as a chief inspector at Scotland Yard. Mr. Fulton, Scout's tutor, stood on the sidelines watching wistfully. Felicia, catching the young teacher's eye, raised a thinly plucked, deeply arched eyebrow and winked. The poor man blushed.

Ginger clucked her tongue. What was she to do with Felicia and her bright-young-thing ways?

Ambrosia, the matriarch of the house, was known publicly as the Dowager Lady Gold. Sitting upright in one of the green velvet wingback chairs, her grey hair was tucked under a feather-rich hat, and her bejewelled fingers clasped her walking stick. Her wrinkled face was stony, showing neither delight nor distaste, but Ginger knew her former grandmother-in-law struggled with Ginger's decision to adopt what she called a "street urchin".

However, Hartigan House was her home, and Ambrosia, after making her original objections known, was wise enough to keep her thoughts on the matter to herself.

Scout played with Boss in the corner by the fireplace. He'd put on weight since joining her family and, though small for his age of nearly twelve, had grown at least four inches. Some had wondered aloud, and not so sensitively at that, why Ginger, if she must adopt, hadn't chosen an infant? Surely, there were plenty of babies around and from better stock?

She couldn't explain how fate had stepped in. When a heart loves, it simply loves unconditionally.

When the music ended, Ginger approached the drinks trolley manned by her butler, Pippins. Of all the people in the room, Ginger had known Clive Pippins the longest and considered the spry blue-eyed septuagenarian to be more like family than a mere employee.

His cornflower-blue eyes nearly disappeared behind folds of skin as he handed her a glass of champagne with a smile.

"Thank you, Pips," she said, and glancing back at Basil, added, "Darling?"

Basil stepped in behind her. "Pippins, I'll have a gin and tonic if you would."

"Certainly, sir."

Basil touched Ginger's elbow then left to join a group of men who'd congregated in one corner and were immersed in what appeared to be a rousing conversation about the stock market.

"Capital, my good fellow," one said.

And another, "I'm making a fortune hardly lifting a finger."

Pushing back an underlying sense of fatigue, Ginger joined Ambrosia, who seemed to be having a hard time not looking put out by their neighbour, Mrs. Schofield, who sat in the next chair.

"How serendipitous that the Adoption Act should come into effect just when your granddaughter decided to take in the stable boy."

Ambrosia's feathers ruffled.

"He was Georgia's *ward*. Not a stable boy."

Ginger's lips twitched at the use of her birth name, which Ambrosia often used when addressing her in formal settings or with people she felt were stationed beneath her, such as their inquisitive neighbour. Mrs. Schofield, her white hair knotted on the top of her head in a Victorian-style bun, had a sparkle of mischief in her eye. Ginger was quite certain the elderly lady enjoyed tormenting her friend.

"And now he's your grandson!"

Ambrosia's wide blue eyes focused on Mrs. Schofield. "You know full well that Georgia was married to my grandson."

"Very well," Mrs. Schofield returned, barely holding on to a chuckle. "*Great*-grandson."

"We're not actually related. As you know."

"Not by blood, but surely by circumstance?"

Ginger felt a twinge of pity for the dowager. "Champagne, Grandmother? I've not touched it yet."

"Yes, please." She held out a leathery hand. "Will you join us?" Then she lowered her voice just enough that Mrs. Schofield could still hear, "Before she talks my ear off."

Ginger bit her lip to hold in a smile and took an empty seat.

Lord and Lady Whitmore, neighbours on

Mallowan Court as well, were amongst the guests. Lord Whitmore, a distinguished-looking gentleman in his sixties, and Ginger shared a confidence—they were both involved with the British secret service, though Ginger had stepped out after the war. It was a fact they both pretended to know nothing about, and anyone in the room would likely be shocked if they knew the truth, including all the members of Ginger's own family.

Lord Whitmore splintered away from his wife, pulled into the grouping of men by the lure of money talk. Lady Whitmore, in her constant effort to hold on to her youth, wore a fashionable turban over short hair. She caught Ginger's eye and, with the lampshade fringe of her gown brushing her calves, eased over to join the ladies.

"Such a lovely party," Lady Whitmore said. "The last party I attended was Lady Roth's birthday party. Were you there? No? Yes, well, don't feel bad about not being invited. The occasion fell flat in the end. There certainly weren't any newspapermen present."

Ginger followed the direction of Lady Whitmore's gaze and grinned at the sight of Mr. Blake Brown from the *Daily News*. Wearing a tweed suit over a slight stomach bulge, the wear-line of a hat now removed from thinning hair, and a camera bag strapped over his shoulder, he was rather hard to miss. Ginger had called the *Daily News* hoping to get a bit of coverage in the social pages. It was a stopgap effort on her part to stop tongues from wagging and to answer, once and for all, the probable awkward questions sure to arise. Though her adoption of Scout Elliot wasn't exactly scandalous, it was most undoubtedly unorthodox and fodder for eager gossipers.

This was probably why Lord and Lady Whitmore had accepted Ginger's invitation. The Whitmores weren't close friends, but living in the immediate vicinity had merited consideration, and Lady Whitmore wasn't one to miss out on social highlights. This party would give her something to jaw about to her friends for weeks.

Ginger excused herself and greeted the journalist.

"Thank you for coming, Mr. Brown. I know it's not your usual type of story."

She and Mr. Brown were acquainted, and though their relationship had started on a rocky footing, Ginger now trusted him—as far as one could trust a reporter.

"Your parties aren't usually normal parties, Mrs. Reed."

Ginger fiddled with the long beads around her neck. The last two events Ginger had hosted, and which Mr. Brown had covered, had involved a dead body. She sincerely hoped that wouldn't be the case tonight.

"I can assure you that I'm doing my best to make sure that everyone leaves here alive."

Ginger, her T-strap shoes tapping along the wooden floors, gracefully made her way to the grand piano in the corner. After motioning to the band to end their set, she tickled the ivory keys. The room, subconsciously aware of the change, quieted.

"Now that I have your attention." Basil and Scout glanced at her, and Ginger nodded subtly for them to join her. "I'd like to make a toast. Please, everyone, get your drinks."

Pippins took the cue and brought over two flutes of champagne, and a glass of ginger beer for Scout.

Once everyone had a drink and faced Ginger, she began, "Thank you, everyone, for joining us as we celebrate the official adoption of our son, Scout." Ginger placed a hand on Scout's thin shoulder and felt a twinge of sympathy as he blushed with embarrassment. Scout *had* grown up on the streets of London, and survival almost always meant remaining invisible and out of sight of the average citizen—ostensibly because it was easier to rob them that way. This party was Ginger and Basil's attempt to get the facts out before the tabloids could run amok with half-truths and falsehoods.

"We are pleased that the British government has begun to legislate in the matter of adoption, for the sake of both the parents and the children. From here on, Scout will be legally known as Master Samuel Reed and affectionately as Scout."

Scout was, in fact, the boy's name given by his natural mother. However, no actual documents reported his birth. Ginger only knew of Scout's birthday because his cousin, Marvin, currently engaged with the Royal Navy, remembered the date. Samuel was a name she, Scout, and Basil had decided upon together.

As if hunching low would disguise him, minimise the pop of the flash pan, or diminish the smoke left in his wake, Mr. Brown slouched about as he snapped photographs.

Though most people in the room were dear friends or family, or at least comfortable acquaintances, there was a notable absence. Basil's parents strongly opposed their son and daughter-in-law's decision to adopt Scout. They found him a threat to the "bloodline" and distribution of family wealth. That was enough for them to have threatened to withhold Basil's inheritance. When they'd learned that their son had chosen to defy them, they had gone on a trip to recover and work out what it would mean for their future. The last

Ginger had heard, they were on a ship headed to South Africa.

Ginger, who'd been unable to conceive, either with her first husband, Daniel, Lord Gold, or with Basil, was just thankful to God that he'd brought Scout into their lives, and that she was now a mother, and they, a family of three.

Basil lifted his glass. "Please join me as we celebrate our good fortune."

A chorus of "hear, hear" resounded as glasses clinked and then were sipped from.

Scout tugged on Ginger's arm. "Can me and Boss go to my room now? It's awful stuffy in here."

Boss, at Scout's feet, wagged his stubby tail and panted with his big doggy smile as if he couldn't agree with Scout's sentiment more.

"It's '*May* Boss and I' and yes, you may."

Ginger grinned as she watched the boy and dog dodge adult bodies and disappear out of the double doors that opened to the entrance and grand staircase. She gave her empty glass to her maid Lizzie, a young, slight lass with mousy-brown hair tucked into a white maid's cap and a pixie-like face who cleaned up after the guests with experienced proficiency. Ginger then nodded to the band to strike up again.

"Make it a quick one," she said.

The introductory notes of "Five Foot Two, Eyes of Blue" played, and Ginger grabbed Basil's hand.

"I love a good Charleston," she said as her heels snapped backward to the beat. Basil held her in his arms and matched her move for move. Ginger laughed heartily. Happiness like this mustn't be taken for granted. One never knew what the next day would bring.

## 2

*T*he marvellous thing about running one's own businesses was that one could arrive late for work if one happened to have had a bit too much champagne the night before.

It was late Saturday morning by the time Ginger parked her lovely creamy-white Crossley in front of her Mayfair office. Boss stared up at her from his spot on the apple-red leather seat with wide-eyed enthusiasm, tail wagging in demonstration of his unadulterated bliss. Ginger patted his black head. "If only humans could learn to enjoy the simple pleasures of each day to the same degree as you, Bossy."

She opened the motorcar door and scooped the small dog into her arms—now that London traffic was so congested, she had to be extra careful with her four-footed charge. Boss was quite used to going to work with Ginger in the mornings. Scout had a hard-enough time focusing on his schooling as it was, and Boss was simply too big a distraction for her son.

That was also before she'd started Lady Gold Investigations. It wasn't always prudent to bring a dog along while on a case, though Boss had come in quite handy at times.

Ginger held the rail and took the three steps down to her office. Once a shoe repair shop, Ginger had had the place cleaned out and renovated, and now it was bright and modern, outfitted with two desks and a sitting area. At the back of the room, a narrow corridor led to a small kitchen and a darkroom. Much of her private investigative business involved following people and snapping photos. Or rather, that was much of what Ginger paid Felicia to do.

"Felicia?"

The door had been unlocked, and the open sign placed in the window, but Felicia's desk remained empty. Ginger lowered Boss to the floor, and his little feet tip-tapped to his wicker bed behind her dark-walnut desk. She removed her gloves and called again, "Felicia?"

A strangled voice reached her. "I'm here."

Ginger heard the flushing sound coming from the

loo, and then shortly after, Felicia's beleaguered form appeared. Apparently Ginger hadn't been the only one to have too much champagne.

"I would've taken a day's leave," Felicia moaned. Her two-toned green day frock with a broad satin drop waist wrinkled as she slumped into her desk chair and motioned toward her typewriter, "but I have this deadline."

Felicia not only worked part-time for Ginger as her secretary and an assistant investigator, but she published short mysteries with a prominent London publisher, who didn't mince words if a manuscript didn't arrive on time.

Ginger kept her jacket on. She didn't plan on staying long and only wanted to pop in.

"It was a fabulous party, though, wasn't it?"

Felicia forced a smile. "It was."

"Any news I need to know about?"

Felicia shook her head. "No new calls."

It'd been a while since Ginger had been called upon for a case. There hadn't even been a suspicious death, which in a city of London's size, happened more than one would think. Basil had had a case or two, but they were easily solved, and her husband, who often brought her in on his investigations as a consultant, hadn't needed her services. Perhaps that was why she'd been feeling sluggish lately. She was bored.

The *Daily News* lay folded on Ginger's desk with the headlines ready: 800 COAL MINERS LOCKED OUT. She let out a sigh of sympathy, snapped the paper open, and flipped to the society pages. Blake Brown hadn't disappointed. A lovely picture of Ginger, Basil, and Scout was followed by a simple announcement of their recent adoption and a story covering the party, naming all the significant attendees. It was exactly what Ginger had hoped it would be.

"There's a pile of post on your desk," Felicia said. "I've sorted it out for you. It's mostly bills."

Ginger picked up the pile. The utilities were due. She'd planned a trip to the bank later and would pay them then. She slipped the envelopes into her handbag.

Boss' soft snore reached Ginger and she grinned. "You don't mind if he stays with you?"

"Of course not. I can take him home if you like. I don't think I'll be staying long."

"That would be wonderful."

Ginger couldn't help herself and scrubbed Boss' neck, rousing him awake. "See you later, big boy. Be good."

Boss licked the top of her hand then promptly rested his chin on his paws and closed his eyes.

Ginger's next stop was her dress shop, Feathers & Flair, which handily, was situated around the corner on

Regent Street. It'd started drizzling in the short time Ginger had been indoors, so she opened her purple floral umbrella for sanctuary. She'd hate for the feather in the ribbon surrounding her cloche hat to wither.

Though comparatively new, Feathers & Flair competed well with the upper-class fashion shops in the city. Ginger carefully followed all the trends coming out of Paris and included the latest designs and fabrics. But she had really introduced a revolutionary concept on the second floor where she presented factory frocks in several sizes. The ability to walk out with a garment on the spur of the moment, and at competitive prices, had won her many customers, especially from the younger set.

Ginger pushed open the glass door, turning at the last minute to loosen the springs on her umbrella and shake off the excess water.

She walked boldly across the polished white marble tiles toward her shop manager at the counter. "Good morning, Madame Roux!"

Madame Roux, a middle-aged woman with dark hair and a straight back, was the model of sophistication and efficiency. Ginger honestly didn't know what she'd do without her and prayed the day she'd need to find a replacement for her shop manager would be long in coming.

"Good morning, Mrs. Reed," Madame Roux returned with a French accent Ginger found delightful. "I thought perhaps we wouldn't see you today. I read about your party in the paper. Was the time good?"

"Yes, very good, and I almost stayed at home today, except that I have to go to the bank. I'm only dropping in to pick up the deposit."

"Oui, I'll get it." Madame Roux glanced across the room. The reflection of electric crystal chandeliers sparkled along high ceilings painted bright white and trimmed with gold. The new girl, Millie, was with Mrs. Bloxham, a demanding repeat customer who was examining a mannequin wearing one of the new spring fashions. "I must be quick."

Ginger followed Madame Roux through the burgundy velvet curtain that divided the back room from the main floor. Emma was bent over a sewing machine in deep concentration, her fingers working feverishly, as her foot pressed the pedal in time. She greeted Ginger without looking up. "Hello, Mrs. Reed."

Ginger smiled, "Hello, Emma." Her young seamstress was very good at what she did, and Ginger had been fortunate to find her before she'd been snatched up by one of her competitors.

Rolls of fabric lined the walls. "A new order of Egyptian fabrics should be arriving soon," Ginger said.

Her comment made Emma pause and glance at Ginger dreamily. "I can't wait to see them." Madame Roux stepped out of the small office with a manilla envelope in her hand. "This is everything from yesterday."

Ginger was pleased with the thickness and glad that she'd invested in a safe.

Her floor assistant, Dorothy West, nearly ran into her as she rushed down the steps from the upper floor.

"Where's the fire, Dorothy?" Ginger asked with a smile.

"I'm so sorry, Mrs. Reed," Dorothy said with flushed cheeks. "It's just that I've got a customer upstairs who wants to try on the hats that are down here."

"Why not just bring her down?"

"She's still browsing and doesn't want to bother with the stairs."

Ginger understood how demanding some customers could be and waved her flustered staff member off. Was it a mistake she'd taken on an inexperienced girl? Ginger wondered. But despite looking like the last person to cross the finish line in a race, Ginger couldn't complain about Dorothy's job performance, though there was a reason she kept Dorothy busy upstairs where her more discerning customers refused to go.

"I don't know," Mrs. Bloxham said. "The fur trim seems out of place in the summer."

Madame Roux purred. "Fur trim is in vogue all year long, Madame Bloxham. Even Hollywood starlets are wearing it."

Ginger smiled at Madame Roux as she smoothly managed her customer. Millie had changed into the outfit worn by the mannequin and was gracefully modelling it across the floor. When the bell over the door announced the entrance of Lady Whitmore, Mrs. Bloxham stared at her potential competitor. She stepped in front of Millie as if to block the interloper's view of the original design. "I'll take it."

"Lady Whitmore," Ginger said. "What a pleasant surprise!"

"I thought I might find you here. I wanted to personally thank you for such a pleasant evening."

"Thank you. And I'm so happy you came."

"Yes, well, it takes a lot to get Lord Whitmore out of the house in the evenings. When he's home, that is. The bank has him working all hours, it seems. In fact, I just dropped in at Barclays—I was in the area—and he'd already left for an early lunch. I've told him he needs to eat a bigger breakfast, at least a piece of kidney with his toast, but he's always in too much of a hurry."

"I'm heading over that way myself," Ginger said. "I'll be sure to say hello if I see him."

After a moment of uncertainty Lady Whitmore responded, "Yes, please do."

Ginger banked at Barclays on Fleet Street, an area known more for the newspapers than anything else. Flanked with tall stone buildings butted together along the length of the street, the roadway bustled with tall black motorcars and double-decker buses. Pedestrians wore hats and long coats as they scurried about, seemingly taking their lives into their hands as they crossed the street.

Ginger spotted Mr. Brown darting to the front door of the *Daily News*, right shoulder weighed down by a camera bag, a well-chewed pencil tucked behind one ear which the newsman had clearly forgotten about when he'd put on his hat. Ginger chuckled and waved, but Mr. Brown had disappeared inside the red-brick building without seeing her. She made a mental note to drop in when she had finished with her errand to thank him in person for the kind story.

The rain hadn't let up, and the droplets had grown heavier. Loud splatting sounds knocked on Ginger's umbrella. The pavements were clogged with people, and Ginger was careful not to jab the passers-by in the eye with the tip of an umbrella rib and tried to avoid the horrible fate herself.

If only the traffic hadn't been so bad and the parking so condensed, she might've found a parking space closer to the bank entrance. Shifting her handbag higher onto her shoulder, Ginger made sure she had a good grip on its contents. With her head down and pressed into the wind, she did what she'd feared and bumped into somebody.

"Oh, please do excuse me," she said, backing up.

"It's quite all—"

The gentleman stopped mid-sentence and stared; his mouth fell open. "Mrs. Reed?"

"Lord Whitmore. This is such a coincidence."

The accidental meeting wouldn't have been quite so awkward if it hadn't been for the *femme*, at least half Lord Whitmore's age, hanging on to his arm and sharing his umbrella.

She pulled away at Ginger's scrutiny. "I'll see you later, George," she said, then rushed inside the residential building beside them.

Lord Whitmore ran a finger between his neck and blue silk ascot tie. "That was my, um, niece."

Ginger blinked at the blatant lie. Not so long ago, during a trying murder case that involved Feathers & Flair, she'd caught Lord Whitmore having an affair. He'd tried to brush it off as part of a cover for his work with the secret service until the lady had turned up dead.

"Such a fluke to run into you, Lord Whitmore. Just minutes ago, I spoke to Lady Whitmore. We were in my shop, and she said she'd been to Barclays to see you, only that you'd taken an early lunch."

Lord Whitmore hunched under his black umbrella and whispered as if they were in a conspiracy together. "Please don't mention this to Sara."

Ginger widened her eyes and smirked. "Why? Does she not know about your *niece*?"

"Of course not. Now, I know you're not as naive as you like to make yourself out to be Mrs. Reed. I understand you're rather a lady of the world."

"What do you mean by that?"

"I've heard that you like to frequent night clubs and even bare a leg or two."

Ginger laughed. "I was working on a murder investigation with my husband, which I'm sure you already know." Ginger snorted at the man's lame attempt to turn the tables. "You can breathe easy, Lord Whitmore. I can keep a secret."

Ginger didn't think it her place to get involved in another couple's marriage, though if Basil were the sort of man—and thank goodness he was not—to wander, she'd hope someone would let her know. As it was, everyone seemed to know about Lord Whitmore's philandering ways, except Lady Whitmore, which was more ironic since she credited herself on being on top of all the gossip, especially amongst the peerage. Ginger felt sorry for her. She was certain Lady Whitmore was the source of much mirth and a topic of gossip herself.

Ginger had become adept at keeping memories of her life in France and the British secret service at bay, but these chance encounters had a way of stirring them up again, along with the myriad of emotions attached to them. Images of Daniel, her late husband, sprang to mind. Her heart warmed as she recollected the last time she'd seen him alive, only days before Captain Smithwick—her heart darkened at the thought of the man she singularly despised— sent Daniel and his regiment on their doomed assignment.

Lord Whitmore continued on to the bank, and Ginger held back so as they didn't appear to be travelling together. Inside Barclays, Lord Whitmore disappeared into one of the offices. She'd heard he'd taken a management position—it wasn't unheard of for a member of the peerage to work as there was such a thing as having one's assets all tied up, even in these prosperous times. On the other hand, Lord Whitmore could've been placed there by the higher-ups at the agency, a notion that tickled Ginger's curiosity. Was

Lord Whitmore on assignment? Was that why he'd pretended to be with a niece?

Feeling rather frazzled, Ginger made her deposit and headed back to Hartigan House. A bath and a nap were in order. She had to remind herself that she was a woman in her thirty-third year and no longer had the stamina she had had in her youth.

## 3

𝒰nlike other mornings, breakfast on a Sunday was a shared family event. Ambrosia dragged Felicia out of bed as if she were still a teenager and not a lady in her early twenties, and Ginger now had Scout to rouse out of bed.

Mrs. Beasley, the cook who was nearly as wide as she was tall, ruled her kitchen like an army sergeant, but the meals were top-notch, and the English breakfast—eggs, bacon, sausages, grilled tomatoes, fried kippers, and kidneys—on display in the morning room buffet was divine.

Ginger poured herself a second cup of coffee then held the pot over Basil's half-empty cup. "Darling?"

"Yes, please," he said. His gaze darted to the newspaper headlines, which reported a bomb threat. "I'm afraid things could get ugly."

Ginger agreed. "The King is certainly unhappy."

"Can we ride after church, Mum?" Scout asked. The stable behind Hartigan House was home to two horses, Ginger's Akhal-Teke, Goldmine, and Basil's Arabian, Sir Blackwell.

"I think that would be splendid," Ginger said, "providing the weather holds up."

The sun broke through fluffy clouds and brightened the morning room. In warmer weather, the French doors were opened to the patio in the back garden. Clement had been busy over the last few weeks preparing the grounds and already, they were blessed with views of luscious red roses, purple tulips, and bright green spring growth on the hedges.

Ginger appreciated that they shared the meal because when it came to churches, Ambrosia and Felicia attended the one in their district, while Ginger, Basil, and Scout drove into the city of London to attend the church of their dear friend Reverend Oliver Hill.

"Mr. Fulton's been attending St. Augustine's lately," Felicia said with a glint in her eye.

Ambrosia harrumphed. "If he's got his eye on you, Felicia, he can look elsewhere."

Felicia pouted. "But why, Grandmama? For being quite desperate to find me a husband, I thought you'd be delighted."

"He's not—"

Felicia finished, "Of the right class?"

"Well, if you want to be on the nose about it, I've heard Countess Hawtrey's son is now unattached."

"You want me to marry a divorcee?"

"For goodness' sake, Felicia. Of course not. Mr. Hawtrey's not divorced. He's only given up on the loose woman he was chasing."

Basil choked on his coffee and quieted a cough in his napkin.

"I don't think I'd like my teacher to marry my aunt," Scout said.

Ambrosia stared at him as if she had not seen him enter the room. "It seems the child and I agree on something."

Pippins tapped on the door before entering. He dipped his chin in Basil's direction. "Sir, telephone for you."

Ginger and Basil shared a look before he left the room for Ginger's study, formerly her late father's, where the telephone had been installed. A telephone call on a Sunday morning could only mean Scotland Yard.

Basil returned with his jaw tight.

Ginger stared up at him and asked, "What is it, love?"

"Lady Whitmore has reported her husband missing."

Ginger was struck at the continued coincidence. She'd gone weeks without even thinking the Whitmore name, and now she couldn't seem to get away from it. "What do you mean, missing?"

"Apparently, he didn't come home after work yesterday. Lady Whitmore said that she wasn't concerned at first because he often works after hours, but when she awoke this morning, he still hadn't returned."

Ginger raised a brow. Though she hadn't mentioned her encounter with Lord Whitmore and his paramour, Basil knew of Lord Whitmore's tendency to look elsewhere for love. Basil seemed to read her mind.

"Lady Whitmore insists that Lord Whitmore is always home on Sunday mornings. She says they never miss a Sunday service. According to Braxton, she really is rather distraught."

"What are you meant to do?" Ginger asked. Basil was a chief inspector who worked at CID, the criminal investigation department, which usually involved murder. But, she recalled, Lord Whitmore wasn't just any wayward fellow, he was secret service.

"I'm going to ask around. Apparently, Lord Whitmore merits more attention than a regular bloke not wanting to face his wife after a night of misbehaving."

"On a Sunday morning?" Ginger asked. Most good citizens would be in church and unavailable for an interview.

"I'll start with Lady Whitmore, and by then, church services will have finished." Basil tilted his head in question. "Would you like to join me?"

Basil often asked Ginger to accompany him on interviews as an unofficial consultant. She had a way of making people relax and, when needed, a knack for catching them off guard.

"Scout, love," Ginger said, giving the boy's head a playful scrub. "You can go to church with Aunt Felicia and Lady Gold."

Though not a blood relative to Ginger, Felicia was her late husband's sister, and as close to a sister to Ginger as her American half-sister, Louisa, back in Boston. Felicia had happily taken on the role of "auntie" to Scout. Ambrosia wasn't quite as pliable and had made it clear she'd like her relationship to Ginger's new son to remain formal.

Scout played his part well. "Oh, Mum, do I have to? Can't I stay and play with Boss and the horses?"

Ginger was pleased that he hadn't dropped his *h*'s and that he'd even dared to argue back. As a member of staff, and even as her ward, Scout wouldn't have dared to do so. This vocal rebellion tickled Ginger—Scout was acting like a true son!

"You can play with them after church, as planned."

Scout pouted as he attacked his boiled egg, and Ginger wondered if he was just trying out his new role as well.

## 4

*B*asil waited, as he often did, as Ginger paused before the mirror by the front entrance to examine her reflection. If it were anyone else, the slight delay would annoy Basil, but he delighted in watching his wife as she smacked lips, added a subdued shade of pink, and with dainty fingers, trained the tips of her red bob to curl neatly over her high cheekbones.

Basil cleared his throat with a look, and Ginger quickly joined him. The Whitmores lived on the other side of Mallowan Court, which meant they could conveniently stroll across the street to see them.

"There's something I should mention," Ginger said as they headed down the cement steps.

"Yes?"

"I ran into Lord Whitmore yesterday on my way to

the bank. I saw Lady Whitmore too. She came into the shop just before I left to run my errand."

"That is coincidental," Basil admitted. He opened the wrought-iron gate at the edge of the front garden. "Is there more?"

One of the many things Basil admired about Ginger was her reluctance to tattle. He'd witnessed the carefully controlled frustration of more than one society lady when Ginger refused to entertain gossip.

"I caught him with another woman," Ginger finally admitted. "It was raining, and they were sharing an umbrella quite intimately."

"I see." Basil wasn't surprised by Ginger's pronouncement. He opened the gate to the Whitmore front garden and waited for Ginger to pass through before closing it.

"I'm assuming Lady Whitmore will be home," Ginger said.

"For all we know, Lord Whitmore has returned with his tail between his legs."

Ginger gave Basil a sideways glance. "You don't seem to have a high regard for Lord Whitmore, love."

"I suppose I'm not a fan of men who wound their wives." Basil grabbed Ginger's gloved hand and kissed it. "But it's more than that. I can't put my finger on it, but he seems ingenuous at times, like he's more than what he presents to the public."

A stern-faced butler answered after Ginger released the thick knocker on the door.

"Good morning," Basil began. "I'm Chief Inspector Basil Reed, and this is my wife, Mrs. Reed. We'd like to see Lady Whitmore."

"Certainly, Chief Inspector. Mrs. Reed." The butler showed them to the sitting room where the decor, never modernised, remained thoroughly Victorian with dark colours, plenty of wood, and walls liberally covered with framed paintings.

Hatless, Lady Whitmore looked smaller and somehow more fragile.

"Thank you for coming, Chief Inspector," she said as she took a chair. She eyed Ginger with a flash of suspicion. "It's good of you to come as well, Mrs. Reed. I've ordered tea."

Basil produced a notebook and a short pencil. "When was the last time you saw your husband, Lady Whitmore?"

"Yesterday morning at breakfast. I stopped at the bank just before lunch to say hello, but he'd left for an early lunch." She glanced at Ginger. "I shopped at Feathers & Flair shortly afterwards."

"Yes," Ginger said. "I hope you found something you liked?"

Lady Whitmore smiled. "Oh, I did. That pink tartan Jean Patou with the grand black silk ribbon on the hip—such a lovely spring frock! Your shop is a cut above the rest, Mrs. Reed. You should be proud."

"Oh, I am. I love the new summer fashions. I can hardly wait for the weather to turn."

"I, as well. I was just saying to Mrs.—"

Basil cleared his voice loudly and shot Ginger a look. How quickly Lady Whitmore had been distracted from her consternation over her missing husband.

Lady Whitmore had the sense to blush.

A maid arrived with a tea tray, and the conversation stilled until the tea was served and the maid retreated.

"I'm sorry, Chief Inspector," Lady Whitmore said after her first sip. "I'm quite used to my husband not being here. My mind can easily skip a beat and forget, for the briefest moments, that his whereabouts are unaccounted for."

"Do you have any idea where Lord Whitmore may have gone?" Basil asked. "Did he have a favourite place to escape to when he was feeling stressed? Friends that he might contact?"

Lady Whitmore returned her teacup to its matching saucer and produced a handkerchief. "That's the thing about my husband. He's quite secretive." She stared blankly out of the window. "I'm afraid I'm not his confidante." She smiled weakly in

Ginger's direction. "We don't all have the enviable marriage that the two of you seem to have." She stared at the handkerchief in her hand, mindlessly twisting it into a rope.

"Is there anything else that is troubling you?" Ginger asked.

Lady Whitmore's chin remained ducked as she spoke. "He seemed, er, not himself recently. Fretting a lot. Forgetful."

"Forgetful?" Basil asked.

"Yes, with little things. Forgetting where he placed his spectacles, not remembering the names of acquaintances. He'd get quite testy about it. I told him I hoped he wasn't losing his mind like Viscount Brimble. They had to take the viscount to their country estate, you know, so that he wouldn't get lost in the city. Permanently, not just for the summer months. It was dreadfully embarrassing for the Brimble family." She looked up ruefully. "George nearly bit my head off for saying so."

Putting his half-empty teacup on the side table, Basil got to his feet. Ginger took his cue and did the same.

"Thank you for your time," Basil said. "We'll continue our investigations and hopefully will quickly locate Lord Whitmore safe and sound."

Lady Whitmore's eyes didn't express the same

hope. "Thank you," she said, then called for the butler to show Ginger and Basil out.

Even though Lady Whitmore was a known gossip, Basil didn't think she'd make up stories about her missing husband for effect. He lowered his chin and spoke in Ginger's direction. "What do you know about Viscount Brimble?"

Ginger answered, "I've only heard Ambrosia mention him on one occasion." They reached the front of Hartigan House, and she continued as Basil opened the gate. "He was diagnosed with early dementia, apparently, but his family insists the viscount simply prefers the quiet and solitude the country affords. However," she continued, "if Lord Whitmore has been afflicted with a weak memory, it could explain his disappearance."

Lord Whitmore didn't appear the type to suddenly lose his way around London, Basil mused. He considered his next move—cases like this one were like strategy games such as chess.

"Lord Whitmore is a grown man," Ginger began, "and in what appears to be an unsatisfactory marriage. If he is starting to grow forgetful, perhaps he just forgot to come home from his dalliance."

Basil dipped his chin. "I suspect your assessment is

correct, but for Lady Whitmore's sake, it wouldn't hurt to have a chat with Mr. Poole, the junior manager at Barclays. He attends St. George's Church. We could catch the last bit of the service and ask him a few questions. According to the officers at the Yard, the bank was the last place anyone could remember seeing Lord Whitmore."

Driving his forest-green Austin 7, Basil pulled onto the grounds of St. George's Church in the City of London. The small chapel built of square stones had a sizable garden with a graveyard, and near the back, a parsonage where the reverend and his family resided.

The square tower faced the main street, and the dome of St. Paul's Cathedral could be spotted through a gap in the buildings across the way. Basil hadn't been much of a churchgoer before he had married Ginger, but he liked the vicar, and that went a long way with him.

Reverend Oliver Hill, with his flaming and untameable curly red hair, stood at the pulpit in his white vestments. Basil and Ginger quietly stepped inside the nave and slipped into an empty pew at the back.

Basil scanned the crowd in search of Mr. Edward Poole, though it was hard to identify someone when all one could see were the backs of heads. However, Basil was acquainted with Mr. Poole and knew the man had early baldness, and during communion, searched for a ring of dark hair surrounding a pinkish-white crown.

Ginger spotted him first, and as everyone rose for the last hymn, nudged Basil's arm. She whispered, "That's him, three rows up, left-hand aisle."

Basil's gaze followed hers until he saw him too.

Oliver gave the benediction, and the quiet ended with the shuffling of feet and light conversation. When Mr. Poole, hat in hand, strolled by, Basil lifted a palm. "Mr. Poole, might I have a word?"

Mr. Poole stared back in confusion. Though they'd attended the same church service every Sunday, they didn't move in the same circles. According to Ginger's accounts, Mr. Poole was a savvy banker, though, and every customer was to be treated like royalty. He quickly recovered his poise. "Good day, Chief Inspector Reed, Mrs. Reed." He extended his hand. "How splendid it is to see you."

"And you, Mr. Poole," Ginger said.

"What can I help you with on Sunday morning?"

"Not to distress you," Basil started, "but a senior manager at your bank, Lord Whitmore in fact, is apparently missing."

"Missing? Really?"

"Yes. Lady Whitmore reported his absence to the police this morning."

"Are you most certain he just hasn't failed to report his whereabouts?"

"No, we're not certain," Basil admitted, "but as a courtesy, I've promised to ask around."

"A dastardly affair!" Deep in thought, Mr. Poole returned his hat to his head, apparently forgetting that he was still inside the church. "I don't know how I can help you, sir. Lord Whitmore left the office yesterday at five o'clock, just after the bank closed."

"Did he normally leave at five?"

"Well, sometimes he left earlier." He stepped forward and lowered his voice. "Lord Whitmore, being a member of polite society, lives by his own rules."

Ginger blinked at the man's frankness.

"Forgive me," Mr. Poole said, his neck growing red at the realisation he might've said too much. "Perhaps I shouldn't have divulged my own feelings. Now, if you'll excuse me, my wife is waiting. I do hope you find your man."

"That was odd," Ginger said, once the man had walked away.

Basil nodded subtly. "Indeed."

"We must say hello to Matilda before we go." Matilda Hill and Oliver were the proud parents of a sweet newborn whom Ginger adored. "Little Margaret is with them."

Basil knew the unusual and trying circumstances

under which Ginger and Matilda had become friends and the unconventional love story between the reverend and his wife. He and Ginger couldn't have been happier for the young couple.

"Would you like to hold her?" Matilda asked, offering up the tiny, swathed infant.

As Ginger accepted the child, the baby stared back at her with big round eyes. After a few moments, the infant's little mouth worked a small O as if in search of her next meal. Ginger handed the baby back. "I think she's hungry."

"She's always hungry," Oliver said. He'd finished shaking everyone's hand as they left and had returned to his wife. "She's going to turn into a tub of lard if we're not careful."

"Would you like to stay for lunch?" Matilda offered. "I can let Mrs. Davies know to make a bit more."

"Thank you so much for the offer," Ginger said, "but I promised Scout I'd go riding with him this afternoon, and Mrs. Beasley is expecting us back."

"How is the young lad?" Oliver asked, his eyes asking more. *Where is he?*

Basil knew Oliver had a special spot in his heart for Scout. Ginger and the vicar had started the Child Wellness Project for street children, and Scout had once been amongst the youngsters who came for the meals it provided. Ginger was quick to reassure her friend. "Scout is well. We sent him to church with Ambrosia since Basil and I had a few other things to attend to."

They said goodbye to Matilda, Ginger cooing over the baby once more. "She's so beautiful."

Oliver chuckled. "Thank God she's taken after her mother!" As Oliver walked them out, he asked, "Is everything all right? I couldn't help but see you talking to Mr. Poole?"

Ginger told him that Lord Whitmore had gone missing. "Do you know him?"

"Only by reputation. He's frequently mentioned in the society pages. Did he and Lady Whitmore not just attend your celebration, Ginger?"

"Yes, they were both there. We did miss you, though."

"I regret we couldn't make it. Little Margaret just couldn't be settled, and we didn't want to leave her with a nanny."

"I quite understand," Ginger said. "Was there something more about Mr. Poole you wished to share?"

Oliver hesitated. "I hate to contribute to gossip, but if it will help you solve your mystery, Mr. Poole had boasted about getting Lord Whitmore's position soon."

hen Lord Whitmore failed to return home by Monday morning, and a telephone call to the bank confirmed that he hadn't shown up for work either, Ginger suggested that she and Basil visit the area on Fleet Street where she'd bumped into Lord Whitmore the previous Saturday.

"Very good idea, love," Basil said. "I'll get my hat."

By the time they reached Fleet Street, the dreary grey skies that had plagued the city for days had cleared. Tulips and daffodils planted in pots by city dwellers turned their colourful heads to the early May sun, petals reaching towards it. Spring was such an exciting and hopeful time of year, Ginger thought. Winter was nicely tucked away, and though the summer temperatures of the United Kingdom were usually moderate, the warmer weather stretched deep into the autumn months.

Ginger often reminisced over the bounty of snow in Boston that she'd enjoyed as a child and preferred the white precipitation to wet. But now, after being back in London for the last three years, even though she'd grown used to the rain, she couldn't stop herself from raising her chin to the warmth and closing her eyes, basking in its delight whilst she could. Unfortunately, the forecast was for more damp skies and cooler temperatures.

"Dear Lord, you're beautiful."

Ginger felt Basil's strong hands grip her waist, and she snapped her painted eyelids open. "Mr. Reed! We're in the middle of the pavement!"

Basil sighed and pulled down on the brim of his hat. "If you wouldn't mind being less adorable then, it would help me tremendously."

Ginger gripped Basil's hand, lifted herself onto her tiptoes, and kissed her husband on the cheek. They'd been married for a year and a half and still felt like newlyweds.

"Remind me to kiss you good and hard when we get home, Mrs. Reed."

Ginger laughed. "I certainly will."

"So, tell me, love, what exactly happened between you and Lord Whitmore? Run me through the steps."

Ginger pointed to the area she'd parked her Crossley, not far from where they now stood, and led Basil across the road and down the opposite pavement.

"People were huddled under umbrellas, and it was difficult not to knock into each other. I was looking down to avoid small puddles."

Ginger, her eyes scanning the building facades, stopped when they reached one with an old unlit gas lamp. "I bumped into Lord Whitmore right here. The lady he was with darted inside that building."

The main door of the building opened, and a man in a trench coat and a trilby hat skipped down the steps. His rugged, good-looking features were tightened in a scowl. Mr. Leo Tipper, a competitor of Blake Brown's, wrote rather scrupulous feature articles for the London News Agency.

Not wanting to be recognised, Ginger turned her back to the journalist. Her mind raced: what was Mr. Tipper doing at the same residential building as Lord Whitmore's supposed niece? It could merely be a coincidence they both lived in the same building, Ginger mused, but her instincts said otherwise. To Ginger's relief, the man turned down the pavement in the opposite direction. Once he was out of earshot, she said to Basil. "That was Mr. Tipper from the London News Agency."

Basil scowled. "I thought I recognised him. What on earth was he doing here?"

"I wondered the same thing."

Basil opened the door for Ginger, and she stepped inside the small foyer. A row of post boxes lined one wall, and though they were each tagged with their owner's name, Ginger and Basil had no way of knowing which one belonged to the blonde, since Lord Whitmore hadn't mentioned her name. There was no tag with the name Tipper either.

"Which one is the caretaker?" Ginger asked.

"I'm going to wager it's the lone flat on the ground floor," Basil said. He headed down the short corridor past the post boxes and beyond the stairs. Basil's assumption proved correct, as a sign that said "Caretaker" was nailed to the door. Basil knocked.

A grandfatherly man wearing loose corduroy trousers and a knitted waistcoat answered the door. The smell of meat pie wafted out, and Ginger's stomach reminded her they were late for lunch.

"I'm Chief Inspector Basil Reed," Basil began. "Can I assume you are the building caretaker?"

"You'd be correct, sir. Mr. Savage at your service."

"I'm looking for an attractive blonde—single, I presume—who lives in one of these flats."

"She has green eyes, a heart-shaped face, and wears a yellow spring jacket," Ginger added.

"Oh, yes. That'd be Gladys, er, Miss Darby, I suspect. Why?" The caretaker's grey brows furrowed with worry. "Is she in trouble?"

"Not at all," Basil said reassuringly. "We think she might know a gentleman who's been reported missing."

Mr. Savage's brows narrowed. "I see, well, she's in flat five, one floor up."

"Thank you," Basil said. "Do you know if Miss Darby is at home?"

Mr. Savage shrugged. "'Ow would I? I can't see the front door from 'ere."

The building caretaker disappeared behind the door, and Ginger followed Basil up one flight of steps. "Mr. Savage didn't seem too keen on the idea that Miss Darby might've been involved with someone," she said.

Basil nodded. "Perhaps he's infatuated."

When they reached the flat, Basil knocked. "Miss Darby?"

When an answer wasn't forthcoming, he knocked again. "Miss Darby? Police. Just a few questions for you."

"I don't hear anyone on the other side of the door," Ginger said. "I don't think she's home."

"I'll send an officer around later to take her to the station," Basil replied.

They headed down a floor and knocked on Mr. Savage's door.

"Miss Darby's not in," Basil said. "Do you have a spare key?"

"Yes, of course. I'll fetch it."

Back upstairs, the three of them went. Mr. Savage unlocked Miss Darby's door, pushed it open, but remained in the hall.

The flat was neat and feminine with floral designs and brightly coloured curtains. The floor outside the closed bathroom door was glossy from water seeping from under the door. A cable trailed through it. Basil cast a glance at Ginger before testing the knob. The door wasn't locked and more water oozed out as Basil pushed it open.

The bathroom was a grouping of white porcelain decorated with touches of pink: the towels, the soaps, and a cluster of lotions. That's where normality ended.

There was a body in the bathtub.

It didn't belong to Miss Darby, however. The bloated figure in the overflowing bath was none other than Lord Whitmore himself.

Oh mercy.

## 6

*L*ord Whitmore's decency was protected by the addition of an unwelcome radio cabinet the size of a breadbox and with a shiny walnut finish. Basil, with gloves on, pulled the plug from the electric socket located just outside the door in the corridor. As many of the buildings in the city had been built long before electricity was discovered, the wiring and power sockets had simply been attached to the wall. Manufacturers often provided long cables to their electrical appliances to ensure that they could reach one of the few power sockets in any room.

Mr. Savage, his round face white as dough, stood behind Ginger and Basil with his eyes locked onto Lord Whitmore's body. "Miss Darby often listens to the wireless whilst bathing," he choked out.

Ginger shot him a look, and Mr. Savage hurried to

explain. "I hear it sometimes as I pass down the corridor."

Basil, his mouth tight, and his eyes grim, said, "Do you have a telephone, Mr. Savage?"

"I do, sir, as I am the caretaker."

"Very good. Do ring Scotland Yard and mention Lord Whitmore's name. And please don't leave the premises before giving a statement."

Mr. Savage darted downstairs, leaving Ginger and Basil alone.

"Act of passion?" Basil said. "Perhaps Miss Darby wasn't pleased with her arrangement any longer."

Recollecting the now-widow's skittish behaviour, Ginger offered, "Or Lady Whitmore had had enough."

"Do you think she knew?"

Ginger arched a brow. "The wife always knows."

"I suppose."

Unlike one would expect, Lord Whitmore's clothing hadn't been discarded in the bathroom. Only a dry white towel hung on one hook. Ginger wrapped her arms across her chest and stepped back into the bedroom. Glimpsing her reflection in the mirror, Ginger admired her powder-blue spring jacket—a new spring line acquisition—with its broad lapels, purple zigzag trim on the flair of the sleeves and the hem, and most notably, the two oversized buttons that fastened it at the waist. After a quick twirl, she perused the rest of the flat.

The twelve-foot ceiling emphasised the large size. In the bedroom, the wardrobe hung open, and Ginger admired Miss Darby's impressive collection of fashionable frocks. Twisted bed sheets attested to a recent session of lovemaking, which was underscored by Lord Whitmore's suit having been carelessly strewn over a lone chair.

Poor Lady Whitmore. Had jealousy driven her to such an act of violence? And if the new widow wasn't guilty of killing her unfaithful husband, she was bound to face many distressing days ahead as she digested the truth. How did one announce such a scandalous situation and curious means of death?

The rhyming pounding of footsteps on the stairs came with a booming male voice. "Just lead the way, sir!"

Ginger and Basil entered the living room just as Superintendent Morris bounded through the door. The man reminded Ginger of a bulldog, but perhaps not as intelligent, with thick jowls and small brown eyes. His trench coat hung over broad, beefy shoulders, and seemed to pinch his armpits.

The man frowned when he spotted Ginger, then directed his attention to Basil.

"Superintendent Morris?" Basil shared a look with

Ginger, who also wondered why the superintendent was there.

"What have we here, Chief Inspector? Is it really Lord Whitmore?"

"It is."

"The higher ups telephoned me right away to get down here and check things out. The posh always get special treatment, don't they?"

Ginger and Basil remained mute. Ginger had given up her title when she married Basil. Though she gladly gave them up, she admitted to missing the privileges that being the wife of a baron had given her. Superintendent Morris gave her a brief look of acknowledgement, but Ginger wasn't certain if he knew he'd slighted her.

His voice carried like a megaphone. "Drowned?"

Basil lowered his chin. "I believe he was electrocuted, sir."

Superintendent Morris plodded towards the bathroom, and Miss Darby's accessories on the dressing table rattled in his wake.

"A blasted wireless! What the dickens was that doing in the bathroom?"

"Some people like to listen to the BBC while they bathe, sir," Basil explained.

"Whatever for? Get in, do the job, and get out, I

always say. What's a dashed waste of time to lounge about like that?"

Ginger rolled her eyes. She and the superintendent had a history of not seeing eye to eye, but after proving her mettle as Basil's unofficial consultant, he'd chosen, reluctantly, to put up with her. Much like a horse puts up with a bird that picks ticks off its back.

"Reed, what do you make of it?"

"I doubt he dropped the wireless on himself, sir."

Unless Lord Whitmore intended to take his own life, Ginger thought, however, it was rather unlikely. A man of his stature most certainly wouldn't plan a scene such as this—dare for his body to be discovered in a strange woman's flat—no, he'd at least contain the mess and subsequent discovery in the privacy of his own home.

The grooves of Superintendent Morris' jowls deepened. "I say it's murder, then?"

Basil nodded. "That's my suspicion."

"Jolly good. Get your men to search the place and take the body to the mortuary."

*Unnecessary instructions*, Ginger thought, since Basil had plenty of experience dealing with crime scenes, but her husband was gracious.

"Yes, sir. I'll keep you informed."

When Superintendent Morris left, it felt as if someone had closed the windows on a blustery day.

Ginger patted Basil's arm. "My hat's off to you, love. He makes me thankful I work for myself."

Basil chuckled. "We can't all have that luxury."

Sergeant Scott, a seasoned officer, had brought the station's French Furet camera, and Constable Braxton, a younger, handsome man, had a fingerprinting kit and a folding measuring stick.

"What exactly should I dust, sir?" Constable Braxton asked. "With all the water about?"

"The door, for a start, and the knob," Basil said.

Constable Braxton opened his kit. "Ten to one, the killer wore gloves."

"Unless it was an act of passion," Ginger said. She could imagine Miss Darby or Lady Whitmore lifting the wireless in a fit of anger and throwing it into the bathtub. Radios were getting smaller and lighter all the time, and one only needed to put their back into it to lift the model in question.

Basil joined Ginger in the living room. "Have you noticed anything askew?"

Ginger shook her head. "There's hardly a speck of dust or a cushion out of place in the living room, and the kitchen is quite tidy. The same can't be said for the bedroom, however. That room looks to be rather well used."

Ginger felt the heat rise to her cheeks at the insinuation of her own words. Of course, the bedroom of a mistress would be made use of more than the kitchen! Ginger presumed that Miss Darby rarely needed to cook for herself and was well acquainted with London's fine dining establishments. That would explain Lord Whitmore's excuses to his wife that he had to work later than Mr. Poole claimed he had.

The ambulance attendant arrived with his men and announced, "Body pick up."

Basil motioned to the bathroom. Constable Braxton walked out with the damaged radio wrapped in a towel. "I'll deliver it to evidence, sir."

"Splendid," Basil said.

After tipping his cap to Ginger, Sergeant Scott turned to Basil and said, "I'll get these photographs developed for you, sir."

Basil nodded. "On my desk as soon as you can."

The sounds of bathwater sloshing about, and the exclamations of the ambulance men as they wrestled a wet and presumably slippery body out of the bathtub reached them, and Ginger bit her lip to stop a smile. *Dreadfully inappropriate.*

"What will you do now?" she asked, diverting her attention from the continuing circus going on behind them.

"I'll get my men on a search for Miss Darby. And a visit to Lady Whitmore is in order—I'll relay her the sad news myself. Perhaps the shock of the situation will rouse some new information. Will you join me?"

"I'd love to, but I promised Scout we'd go riding this afternoon, now that the weather has cleared," Ginger said. "You'll keep me apprised."

"Indeed. I'll drop you off at home. But first, I'd like to have a little chat with the caretaker."

The ambulance men succeeded in their mission and pushed the gurney out of the flat into the corridor, water dripping in their wake. Their efforts down the stairs were hard to watch, and Ginger was thankful they were only one floor up. Mr. Savage stared at the spectacle with a deep frown.

Basil approached the caretaker.

"It goes without saying that no one is to go into Miss Darby's flat, not even the lady herself. It's now a crime scene, and I've locked it up. Please tell Miss Darby to contact me when she returns." For Mr. Savage's convenience, Basil gave him a card with the number of Scotland Yard on it.

Mr. Savage slid the card into his shirt pocket. "The young lady'll be in for a 'uge shock, won't she?"

"How well do you know Miss Darby?" Basil asked.

Mr. Savage's neck reddened. "I don't know what you're implying."

"I'm not implying anything at all, Mr. Savage. It's a simple question."

Ginger thought Mr. Savage rather quick to assume the question was in any way suggestive.

"She's a tenant, like the others," Mr. Savage replied. "Everyone keeps to themselves."

Ginger shifted the strap of her handbag higher over her shoulder. "When did Miss Darby move into the building?"

"Oh, four or five months ago? I'd 'ave to check the record."

Ginger had a feeling that Mr. Savage remembered, to the day, when Miss Darby had moved in. His infatuation pulsed like a beacon.

"Does she have many friends?" Ginger continued. "Or visitors other than Lord Whitmore?"

"It's not like me to spy, madam." A fleck of spittle flew from the caretaker's lips, and Ginger took a small step back.

"You do notice people coming and going, don't you?" Basil pressed. "As you go about your managerial duties?"

"Like I said, the tenants keep to themselves. Leave for work in the mornings, return for tea, that type of thing. I fix broken light bulbs and ring for a plumber from time to time."

Basil gave him a tight smile. "Thank you, Mr. Savage. If you see anything suspicious, please do ring the police right away."

.  .  .

THIS WAS the worst part of his job, Basil thought—informing family members that a loved one had died. At least he had Braxton standing with him for moral support.

The Whitmore butler answered the door.

"Good afternoon, Chief Inspector."

"Good afternoon, Maurice." Basil motioned towards Braxton. "This is Constable Braxton. Is Lady Whitmore available? I'm afraid it's a matter of urgency."

The butler directed them to the sitting room, and soon afterwards Lady Whitmore joined them.

"Is it George? Have you found him?"

Basil stood, hat in hand. "Lady Whitmore, I'm afraid the news isn't good."

A handkerchief flew to her mouth. "Oh my." Her knees buckled, and Braxton took quick strides to support her before she hit the floor and helped her to the nearest chair.

"Summon Maurice," Basil said, "and have him bring Lady Whitmore a brandy."

Lady Whitmore stared up with a wild expression. "What happened to him? Was it a car crash? You must tell me."

Basil inhaled deeply and let out a slow breath. It

was one thing to deliver news of a fellow's death, and another to have to relay the unsavoury circumstances.

"I'm afraid your husband passed away as a result of electrocution."

Lady Whitmore's brow buckled. "Electrocution? However so?"

Basil cleared his throat. "It happened in a bathtub."

Lady Whitmore's eyes stared back blankly. Then, as realisation dawned, a wave of crimson flushed her pale face. She covered her face with both hands. "The humiliation never ends!"

Braxton's arrival with a glass of brandy, was just in the nick of time, Basil thought.

"Here you are, Lady Whitmore," Braxton handed the new widow the tumbler. "Your man was going to present it on a tray, but I thought that it would be quicker if I just brought it straight to you."

Basil nodded his appreciation.

Lady Whitmore took a small sip, swallowed, then took several longer sips in a row before dabbing her mouth with the well-used handkerchief. "Thank you, Constable."

She straightened her back and focused on Basil. "Tell me every detail. I need to know the extent of the scandal, so I can prepare myself. It's sure to hit all the papers and my peers will never let me forget my reproach."

"Very well, but be assured, I'm doing all I can to keep the details from the papers. It appears your husband had a mistress—"

"That explains all the late nights, I suppose, and early lunches." Her gaze drilled into his. "He had one Saturday. I was at the bank, you know. Good heavens, what a laughingstock I've become."

"This isn't your fault," Basil said. "You have nothing of which to be ashamed." Unless, of course, he thought to himself, Lady Whitmore had taken justice into her own hands.

The scorn felt by the new widow was evident in the lines on her face. "I know your father is an Honourable, Chief Inspector, and your wife a former Lady, so surely your condescension is accidental. My life is ruined. Now please, tell me the rest of what you know."

Basil glanced at Braxton, who shrugged subtly in response to Basil's chastisement. Basil knew he had to tread softly but just how was that possible, given the facts?

"Lady Whitmore, your husband's body was found in the flat belonging to a lady—"

"Woman! Not a lady. What's her name? You might as well tell me as I'm sure I'll be told about her before too long."

"The woman's name is Miss Gladys Darby. Lord

59

Whitmore was in the bathtub, alone," Basil thought it pertinent to add that, "except for the presence of a wireless on top of him."

"A wireless? Did it fall in?"

"The crime scene is still under investigation."

"Crime?" Lady Whitmore mused. Her eyes shrunk into worried knots. "My husband was murdered?"

"I'm afraid so."

"Good heavens."

Basil eased into the chair nearest Lady Whitmore. "Can you make an account of your husband's friends?

"George didn't have a wide circle of friends. He was rather a recluse, you could say."

Basil pressed on. "When he wasn't at home or at work, where did he go? Did he have a favourite drinking establishment?"

"He always said he needed to keep busy, which is why he took that job at the bank." Lady Whitmore stared blankly across the room. "You could ask Mr. Poole. Perhaps he had drinking friends there." Releasing a sad sigh, she added, "After twenty-two years, it seems I didn't know my husband well at all."

It wasn't unheard of for couples to grow apart as the years dragged on, Basil supposed.

"Please forgive me, but I have to ask you: where were you this morning?"

Lady Whitmore's look of scorn returned. "You can't be serious?"

"I'm afraid I am. Please retrace your steps."

Lady Whitmore took another sip of her brandy, and Basil noted it was nearly empty. Lady Whitmore did as well and stared up at Braxton, who'd remained stationed at the door. "Constable, would you mind fetching me another?"

Basil nodded his consent, and Braxton disappeared.

After a breath, Lady Whitmore started, "When George, once again, failed to show for breakfast, I asked Maurice to look for him. We have our own rooms, you see, so I didn't know if George had come home or not. Unfortunately, he had not. I've not left the house all day. Maurice can vouch for me."

"What about Saturday?" Basil asked. "What did you do on that day?"

"I had my driver take me to Harrods, a nice way to spend a few hours. After that, I dropped in at the bank, but as you know, George had gone out. Then I went to Feathers & Flair. Mrs. Reed spoke to me there. And then, I came home—I always host a bridge game on Saturday afternoons. After that, I waited for George to come home for dinner, and well, the rest you know."

Basil had taken out his notepad and jotted down

the details. "Do you recall what time it was when you left Barclays?"

Lady Whitmore let out a huff. "I think it was around a quarter past eleven. Well before the lunch hour. You can ask that Mr. Poole. I was quite annoyed with him over it all."

"Lady Whitmore, I'm sorry to have ask you so many questions at this distressing time, but please account for your actions yesterday."

"Sunday? Well, I couldn't very well go to church on my own could I? How would that appear, with my husband not accounted for? I was on my last nerve, and I admit, I let my imagination get away on me. I rang the police."

Basil nodded and jotted down notes as his mind took in this new information. If, as Ginger had surmised, Lady Whitmore knew more than she'd let on, she might have slipped up to Miss Darby's flat this morning and found her husband in the bathtub. Perhaps Miss Darby had failed to lock the front door, and in a fit of indignant rage, Lady Whitmore could have thrown the radio in. The butler could easily have been bought off to provide an alibi, or perhaps he was unduly loyal to his mistress.

It wouldn't be the first time a jilted wife had killed her husband.

## 7

Ginger, about to head upstairs to the library to check on the status of Scout's lesson and if he'd soon be ready to saddle up, found Felicia and Mr. Fulton standing at the bottom of the staircase. Mr. Fulton leaned casually on one rail, while Felicia's arms draped languidly along the other.

Despite the coolness in the air at Hartigan House, Felicia wore a sleeveless summer frock. Adorable as it was with a sailboat neckline and pleated skirt, it didn't suit the chilly, dreary May weather.

"As a mystery writer," Felicia was saying, "of course, I've read everything by Agatha Christie, G.K. Chesterton, and Sir Arthur Conan Doyle."

Mr. Fulton held his briefcase in one hand and cradled his hat in the other. At least he was wearing a trench coat. From Ginger's position near the sitting room, she could see the goose pimples on Felicia's arms.

"I enjoy a good mystery myself, on occasion, Miss Gold," Mr. Fulton said, obligingly. "And I quite admire the fact that you're a published author."

"Only mysteries," Felicia said, "I'm hardly Virginia Woolf."

"Don't undersell yourself, miss. I'm acquainted with plenty of students who'd die to be in your shoes."

Felicia batted her lashes. "I imagine you like to read highly intellectual books."

"Well—"

"Don't deny it," Felicia's look challenged him. "What book do you currently have your nose in?"

Mr. Fulton smirked. *Economic Calculation in the Socialist Commonwealth* by Ludwig von Mises."

Ginger was familiar with the book, a top seller a few years earlier. Mr. von Mises' view was that socialism couldn't work and was destined to collapse in chaos.

Felicia's jaw dropped, and her eyes filled with sudden hopelessness. Ginger doubted she'd even heard the term "socialist calculation" before, much less read a book on the topic.

Mr. Fulton noticed Felicia's change of demeanour

and quickly added, "It's dreadfully boring. It helps me to fall asleep at night."

Doubting that Scout would've remained upstairs on his own, Ginger popped into the sitting room where her son and her beloved dog often played. A favourite of Ginger's, the room was warmly decorated with matching armchairs and a settee facing a large stone fireplace. A Waterhouse painting—*The Mermaid*—was prominently featured over the hearth, the long red locks of the bathing beauty concealing the mythical creature's innocence. The coals in the fireplace had dimmed to grey.

Ambrosia sat poker straight, her wrinkled fingers, heavy with gem-filled rings, firmly gripping the silver head of her walking stick. She wore a fur shawl over her shoulders and a scowl on her wrinkled face.

"Hello, Grandmother," Ginger said.

The wrinkles around Ambrosia's lips tightened. "Ginger."

Feeling a wave of fatigue, Ginger slumped in the chair beside her, unbuckled the double T-straps of her red leather Italian shoes, letting them fall to the Persian carpet, and raised her feet to the ottoman. Boss, pushing one of the double doors open with his black nose, scampered into the room, and jumped onto her lap.

"Well, hello there, Bossy," Ginger said, scrubbing the dog's neck as he kissed her hand. "What have you been up to today? Very busy with important projects, I bet. And no Scout about?"

Ambrosia snorted at Ginger's frivolity.

"What is it, Grandmother? You look like you swallowed a bad egg."

"Besides the fact that I have icicles dripping from my nose like a street beggar?"

"It's a little chilly, I admit," Ginger said. "The next load of coal should arrive soon. In the meantime, you can make use of the blanket hanging on the back of your chair."

Ambrosia harrumphed, and Ginger got the impression that she wasn't physically uncomfortable, but rather enjoyed complaining.

"Not only that," Ambrosia said sharply, "Felicia is trifling with a *teacher*."

So, Ambrosia had witnessed the playful bantering between the two young people. Ginger felt compelled to come to the tutor's defence.

"Mr. Fulton will soon be a university professor and a perfectly acceptable match."

Ambrosia shivered for effect. "I've introduced her to many charming young men of good breeding and class. I swear she spurns them all just to spite me."

"Now, why would she do that?"

"Because she's a rebellious young thing. I'm worried about her, Ginger, truly worried. She's going to end up in disgrace or married to a commoner."

Ginger wasn't sure which situation Ambrosia considered worse: unwed motherhood or marriage to a commoner.

Ginger rang the bell and asked Lizzie to add more coal to the fire. "And a pot of tea for the Dowager Lady Gold."

"None for you, madam?" Lizzie asked.

"No, thank you. I promised Scout I'd go riding with him this afternoon. Do you know where he is?"

"I believe he's already outdoors, madam."

Ginger placed Boss on the carpet and hoisted herself to her feet. "I'll go and put on my jodhpurs then."

"Would you like me to come up to assist, madam?"

Ginger was going to decline but then thought better of it. "If you would. Perhaps Langley could bring the tea."

It appeared that Mr. Fulton had departed since the little tête à tête had ended, and the staircase was clear. Boss followed Ginger upstairs, but instead of heading toward Ginger and Basil's room, he turned into the library. Felicia had shifted a chair close to the low

67

embers of the fireplace and had swaddled herself in a blanket. When she saw Ginger staring at her, she quipped, "I'm tempted to catch the next aeroplane to the south of France."

"You hate flying."

"Of course, I do. It's not natural. When is the coal going to arrive?"

"I don't know. I thought it was coming this morning."

"Mr. Fulton says the coal miners are unhappy. They don't want to work shorter hours for less money."

"Who would?"

"The miners have been locked out. You know what that means? We'll never get our coal!"

"Good thing you have that warm blanket."

"Ginger! I'm serious. We can't live like this."

"You looked rather warm when you were chatting with Mr. Fulton on the staircase."

Felicia grinned, and the circles of her cheeks reddened. "He's a brilliant man, you know, and I find him rather attractive, don't you?"

Ginger shrugged. Now that she had Basil, she didn't take note of other men. "I suppose so. You've got Ambrosia in a tizzy."

"I've always got Grandmama in a tizzy. Between you and me, I'm what keeps her alive. Her heart would likely stop ticking if she didn't have her mini scandals to fret over."

"Felicia!"

She laughed. "It's true, and you know it."

To hide the smile that threatened, Ginger pivoted out of the room. She didn't want to give Felicia any ammunition. The girl was far too powerful as it was.

Lizzie had Ginger's riding outfit laid out on the top of the bed when Ginger sauntered in. "Lizzie, you're a gem."

"Thank you, madam. Can I take your jacket?"

Ginger turned her back to Lizzie and released her arms. "Are you warm enough in the kitchen?"

"There's still plenty of wood for the stove, though if we don't get more coal soon, we'll be eating tinned meats."

Ginger shuddered. After her work in the war, she'd sworn she'd never eat meat from a tin again in her life.

Ginger dropped her dirty clothes to the floor, and Lizzie swooped them up.

"How is your family?" Ginger asked as she slipped into her jodhpurs. With the miners locked out, Hartigan House wouldn't be the only residence to deal with a shortage. "Have you enough coal?"

"There are plenty of bodies to keep our little flat warm," Lizzie said. Ginger couldn't tell if Lizzie was making light of a bad situation or not, but it wasn't like

Ginger had any coal to give her or any way of procuring her some.

THE SMALL STABLE in the back garden of Hartigan House had been unused and neglected for over a decade before Ginger returned to London in '23. Shortly afterwards, and during a rather tragic and challenging case involving horse racing, Ginger had been introduced to the exotic equine breed from Turkmenistan called Akhal-Teke. These gorgeous horses were not only known for speed, endurance, and intelligence but also their coats had a very particular and distinctive metallic sheen.

Goldmine was of the blond variety, and when the sun glistened off his coat, the creature appeared otherworldly. Goldmine never failed to turn heads.

Ginger wasn't surprised to find Scout already brushing down the two geldings, the second being Basil's Arabian, Sir Blackwell. As her ward, he'd taken his duties of caring for the stables and the horses seriously, and now as her son, even more so. She'd taught him how to ride, and Scout had proven to be a natural.

The stable smelled of horse sweat, hay, and dung, which to Ginger was a comforting scent. She pressed her cheek into Goldmine's neck as she stroked his long nose.

"How are you doing, big fella?"

"I've got them both ready for the saddles," Scout said. He lifted one off its brackets, his back straining under the weight. Ginger grasped an edge, gave the lad a hand to lift it onto the back of Sir Blackwell, and left him to attend to the horse's straps and stirrups. Then, Ginger expertly saddled up Goldmine. She felt rather warm after the effort—a nice change from the chilly atmosphere inside the house.

They headed on their usual route to Kensington Gardens, a place that had both good and bad memories for Ginger. The bad involved a body, and the good centred on Basil's proposal of marriage. The latter made up for the former a hundred-fold.

Still, spring was such a lovely time of year and especially so in the grand gardens of Kensington. The palace itself sprawled out in the distance like a giant fortress, its dark stones glistening from the earlier rain. Majestic rose gardens, fit for the king, bordered vast lawns, deeply green with new growth. Birds made their nests in the gatherings of birch and chestnut trees, and fellow riders and strollers meandered along the paths into Hyde Park.

"How was your lesson with Mr. Fulton?" Ginger asked.

"Good. He's quite clever, you know."

Ginger chuckled. "I wouldn't have asked him to be your tutor if he wasn't."

"We talked a lot about the Communist Party in Britain."

Ginger was astonished. Scout wasn't even twelve years old and had never shown an interest in politics. "That's quite a grand topic. How did you get onto that?"

"It's in the newspapers. I read them sometimes, after you and Father leave."

Ginger's heart warmed at Scout's use of the familial term "Father" for Basil. The new title and relationship position had been awkward for both at the beginning.

"Mostly the funnies," Scout continued. "But I saw something about the Reds which confused me, so I asked Mr. Fulton about it."

"And what did Mr. Fulton say?"

"The upper classes don't fancy it. They're afraid the Bolsheviks will take over and steal their freedoms like they did in Russia."

Ginger pinched her lips, noting how Scout classified himself as not amongst the upper classes of which he was now a part.

"It's not only the upper classes who lose out, I suspect," Ginger said.

"People will believe anything when they're 'ungry

and tired, and communist propaganda can be made to sound like an answer to their problems."

Ginger cast a quick sideways glance at Scout. He'd dropped an *H*, but that was the only indication that he'd once been a street urchin. He sounded educated and intelligent, and Ginger made a note to herself to commend Mr. Fulton. Perhaps give him a raise.

Apparently quite enthralled with the topic, Scout chatted on. "I know what it's like to be 'ungry and tired, Mum, and if someone told me that everything would change if I became a communist, I might've joined. Like those miners. Mr. Fulton says, if they don't get what they want, they might run to join the Communist Party."

"Well, I certainly hope not. And it's *h*ungry, not 'ungry."

"Sorry, Mum. *H*ungry. Mr. Fulton says Bolsheviks are everywhere, even London."

The fear of the spread of communism was a growing phenomenon in Great Britain, and Ginger had her own concerns, but she didn't want her son to be weighed down by the potential threat of political oppression. Britain had just fought and won the war to end all wars. For the sake of her son's future, she prayed this Bolshevik nonsense would soon fade.

Though Ginger was quite capable of dismounting Goldmine on her own, she accepted Clement's gracious and expected assistance upon their return. His full face was pinched with worry and her heart immediately jumped.

"Is everything all right in the house?" Her first thought was for dear old Pippins, since had anything untoward happened to the staff or her family members, it would be Pippins who'd be watching for her to deliver the news.

"Yes, madam," Clement said as her boots reached the ground. "Quite all right."

Ginger's intuition wouldn't let her go, and she felt the need to probe her gardener. "Are you quite all right?"

Clement's gaze moved to Scout, who'd easily hopped off his mount and had already led the Arabian back to the stable to remove its saddle and reins and brush the animal down.

"You 'eard 'ow the miners in County Durham were locked out?"

"Yes."

"Well, me nephew's one of 'em, me late sister's lad." He glanced up at Ginger with a tentative stare. "'E's come to see me, with 'is wife and little 'un."

"They're here at Hartigan House?"

"Yes, madam. 'E didn't tell me 'e was comin'. They're sittin' at the staff table, wantin' me 'elp."

"I see. Well, do put them up in the attic as your

guests." Ginger couldn't turn a member of Clement's family away, and besides, there was an infant to consider.

"Thank you, madam. God Bless you."

When Clement failed to step away, Ginger asked, "Is there something else?"

"Madam, I 'ope I'm not being too forward, and you've been so generous already, but should you be thinkin' of takin' on someone to replace the young master?"

Scout walked out of the stable at that moment.

"Would you like me to cool Goldmine down for you, Mum?"

Ginger smiled and handed Scout the reins. "That would be tremendous."

She turned back to Clement and considered his request. When Scout was Ginger's ward, he had lived in the attic with the servants and helped both Clement with the gardening and Mrs. Beasley in the kitchen. Ginger hadn't employed a replacement since she'd brought him into the house as her son.

"With summer coming on, I suppose you could use a bit of help?" Ginger asked.

"Yes, madam, my nephew - 'arold Bronson's 'is name – would be useful to me, and his missus, Angela, can 'elp in the kitchen when the baby's sleeping, at least."

"Very well, you may offer your nephew and his wife the positions. I'll let you see to them getting settled, and we can make introductions later."

Ginger would be pleased to meet Mr. and Mrs. Bronson, but first, she needed a bath. It wouldn't do for her to smell equine.

## 8

$S$cotland Yard was composed of two impressive brick buildings on Victoria Embankment overlooking the River Thames. Everything to do with all manner of police work found itself routed through there, including laboratory testing and post-mortem examinations. It would take some time for the reports to come back and for the autopsy to be performed, but in this instance, Basil suspected that the pathologist wouldn't find out any more than Basil already knew. Whitmore's death had been caused by the cessation of the heart due to the introduction of an excessive electrical current.

On the day after the body was discovered, Basil gave Braxton a new task. "See what you can find out about the Whitmores' finances. I doubt it'll have any bearing on why he was killed, but it's good to rule it out. Money's a chief motive amongst thieves and murderers."

"Yes, sir."

Disappearing into his office, Basil removed his long coat and trilby and hung them on the coat rack in the corner. His space was small but efficient—the only furniture a simple desk and a filing cabinet—but he had something most officers in the building couldn't boast about—a window. He couldn't see much, only the brick wall of the neighbouring building and a corner of the motorcar parking area, but he liked to see the light of day, even if it was mostly the gloomy London fog.

Unfortunately, the light wasn't enough to keep the broadleaved houseplant sitting on the cabinet happy. A gift from a grateful citizen, Basil tried to remember to water it, but the small task simply slipped his mind, especially during a perplexing case.

The moments that Basil found the hardest were those where he found himself waiting for others to complete their jobs. He wished he could do everything himself—laboratory tests, fingerprinting, the autopsy. Then he could be sure it was done promptly. As it was, he depended on the expertise and the timetables of others.

Basil shuffled papers on his desk and reviewed his notes. To get to Lord Whitmore's killer, he had to get into Lord Whitmore's world. Who was Lord Whitmore? Who were his friends and associates? His wife wasn't very useful on that account. Basil couldn't be too sure if she was sincere in her lack of knowledge, or if she had been purposely vague.

Along with Mr. Poole, Basil wanted to speak to Miss Darby, but sitting at his desk waiting around would be a waste of time. He collected his hat, leaving the trench coat hanging, and headed down the corridor to make his escape. Just as he got to the reception area, Sergeant Scott entered with a perturbed-looking, if attractive, young lady, and ushered her in.

"Chief Inspector Reed," Scott said on seeing him. "This is Miss Darby."

Miss Darby patted at the bottom waves of her blonde bob fitted neatly under a cloche hat—a fashion term Basil had learned from Ginger. Her expression softened when her eyes landed on his face, her gaze moving head to toe with a look of appreciation. Basil empathised with his female counterparts, who were physically assessed in such a predatory manner daily.

"Miss Darby," he said. "Please accompany me to my office."

Her lips, thick with dark red lipstick, curled upwards. "With pleasure, Chief Inspector."

Basil appealed to Scott with a look. "Please join us, Sergeant."

With an exaggerated wiggle of her hips, Miss

Darby responded to Basil's wave to enter his office before him. She took the wooden ladder-backed chair that faced his desk and crossed her legs, revealing the dark seam at the back of her stockings, like a showgirl. Basil pulled at his tie as he forced his eyes to look elsewhere and took his seat in his worn leather office chair. Scott stationed himself at the door like a sentry, both men keen to not underestimate a woman like Miss Darby, the mistress of a lord.

"Would you like some tea, Miss Darby?" Basil offered.

Miss Darby's wide-eyed gaze flittered about the office. "A glass of water would do."

Basil nodded at Scott, who disappeared to fetch the water.

Miss Darby smacked her lips, then said, "Why am I here, Chief Inspector? Your officers were rudely vague about their reasons for hauling me in. I've broken no laws."

"Just to confirm, Miss Darby," Basil began, "you reside at twenty-one Fleet Street, here in London."

"I do."

"You've been known to keep the company of Lord George Whitmore."

A careful smirk followed. "I have."

Basil had the feeling Lord Whitmore wasn't the only gentleman whose company she'd kept.

"When was the last time you saw Lord Whitmore?"

Miss Darby cocked her head and fluttered thick eyelashes. "I'd rather not say. He's a married man, as you know. I'm the soul of discretion."

Scott returned with the glass of water. Miss Darby took a dainty sip, then to Basil's astonishment, she rose from her chair, glided across the small room, and poured the rest into the dying plant. She clucked her tongue. "So unnecessarily neglectful, Chief Inspector."

She made a show of walking back to her chair, lowered herself, and crossed her legs, bouncing the top one playfully.

Basil wasn't impressed. "Miss Darby, this is a serious matter."

Miss Darby pouted. "Men go 'missing' all the time. I'm sure he only needed a break from that demanding donkey of a wife."

Basil gaped at Miss Darby's rudeness.

"Oh, don't be so prudish," Miss Darby responded. "Not all men are devoted to their wives, obviously. I'm sure George will materialise when he's good and ready."

"Lord Whitmore is dead."

Basil hadn't meant to be so abrupt, but the shock that rippled across Miss Darby's features was satisfying to witness.

She jumped immediately to denial. "No, he's not. I just saw him this morning. Perfectly alive. He came for a . . . er . . . visit, for...er... a couple of nights."

"Lord Whitmore was in your company since Saturday."

Miss Darby nodded.

Basil felt a pinch of remorse. "His body was discovered later this morning."

Miss Darby's round eyes began to glisten. "Surely not. Where?"

"In your flat, miss."

Miss Darby's jaw dropped, and Basil mused at her speechlessness. The woman was either genuinely shocked or a fine actress.

He dropped the next bomb. "Furthermore, he was murdered."

Miss Darby's shoulders slumped, and her gloved hand slapped her mouth. "No! It can't be. Why would anyone want to kill Lord Whitmore?"

"That is what I intend to find out."

Miss Darby made a show of wiping her tears, managing somehow to do so without smudging her makeup. She lowered her chin and stared up at Basil through damp eyelashes. "H-how?"

Basil was pleased to keep the evidence to himself.

"Miss Darby, please recount your steps of your 'visitation' with Lord Whitmore."

Miss Darby sniffed, narrowed her eyes, and shot Basil an accusing look. "Yes, I imagine a woman of my reputation would be considered your first suspect."

"The man died in your flat, madam."

"I can assure you that I had nothing to do with it."

"Please, Miss Darby, do oblige me."

"Very well. Lord Whitmore and I had a very pleasant weekend together. He was rather tired of his prissy wife, you know. I had a hair appointment at my salon this morning, so I left, letting George know he was welcome to stay as long as he wished."

"And you were gone for the whole morning?"

"I was in a chair getting my hair cut, coloured, and styled." Miss Darby unnecessarily removed her hat to show off the hairdresser's work. She patted loose strands of glossy, honey-blonde hair. "I told her to make me look like Mary Pickford. What do you think?"

"Very nice, Miss Darby. What time was your hair appointment?"

"Ten o'clock."

"In your estimation, was Lord Whitmore acting strangely?"

A neatly arched brow rose higher. "Strangely, how?"

"Forgetful? Missing rendezvous times?"

"Well, Chief Inspector, I have to admit that I honestly didn't know Lord Whitmore that well." She stared back wryly. "But, he was very particular to meet me in a timely fashion; I can assure you of that."

Basil's tie felt inexplicably tight and he ran a finger around his collar to loosen it. "I see. Please give the name of the salon and the stylist to Sergeant Scott on your way out."

"I can go?"

Basil nodded. "But don't leave London without talking to me about it first."

"Ooh, Chief Inspector Reed." Miss Darby ran a long fingernail across her lips. "I'm happy to be on your leash." She sashayed out of Basil's office and left a noticeable vacuum in her wake.

Basil let out a long, hot breath and rubbed the back of his neck. Miss Darby was the epitome of a femme fatale, and though the shock she showed upon hearing the news seemed real, she could be a well-practiced actress. Her profession would call for certain skills that made men believe she felt about them in ways she likely did not. Basil had no problem imagining Gladys Darby picking up the wireless and saying a dramatic and morbid goodbye to Lord Whitmore before rushing to her hair appointment.

*A*fter Ginger's ride with Scout, she did something she rarely ever did. She had a nap. And quite unintentionally, at that. She'd undressed, bathed and, undecided about what to wear for the rest of the day, simply lay on her bed, propped up against large pillows to contemplate. This bedroom had been hers as a child, before her father had whisked her away to Boston and married her stepmother, Sally. It had since been decorated a couple of times—most recently when she'd returned as the heiress and owner of Hartigan House. She found the lightness of the gold and white tones of the decor pleasant to the eye. The striped fabric of the armchairs near the long windows and the lines in the geometric patterns of the wallpaper were an artistic contrast to the ornate wood of the bed frame, wardrobe, and chests of drawers. An old gramophone sat in one corner next to Ginger's full-size, wood-trimmed oval mirror. The floor was spacious enough to dance with Basil—an enjoyable prelude to an evening of romance.

Boss had pushed on the door, which she hadn't closed all the way, with his black paw and joined her on the bed, curling up for warmth beside her. She stroked his fur. "I'm sure more coal will arrive soon, Bossy. Next year I'll make sure that Clement orders enough to last until July!"

The next thing Ginger knew, she was awakened to Boss' wet nose nudging her neck as if he had a sixth sense she was needed somewhere.

Where?

She blinked back at the sense of lost time, momentarily unsure of the day. Was it morning? No, the light coming through the windows was too low. No, it was later in the afternoon, she remembered with mild self-chastisement.

She'd dreamt. What was it now? If felt important. She'd been rummaging through her clothes hanging in the wardrobe. That made sense, as she'd fallen asleep thinking about her options hanging within.

Only it wasn't her wardrobe. The frocks hanging within weren't her frocks.

Whose were they then?

Did it matter?

No. It was just a silly dream. For the briefest moment, she considered ringing the bell for Lizzie. Her maid could pick out something for her to wear, but that would take more time than Ginger had. Swinging her legs off the bed, she stood before her wardrobe, the doors still opened from her first effort. The gowns and frocks were plentiful, and it was difficult to move them about to view her options. She either had to rid herself of some items she wore infrequently or simply must purchase a second wardrobe!

Ginger chose a lemon-yellow skirt with a matching short jacket that tied in a neat little bow around the neck and paired the combination with a white blouse. The skirt hung rather snugly around her hips and flounced out in waves along the hemline, just below her knees. As she slipped into it, an image flashed through her mind. She recalled what had bothered her from her dream.

Quickly stepping into a pair of matching yellow pumps, Ginger hurried down the staircase, Boss following excitedly.

She passed Lizzie in the entranceway as she headed down the corridor, her pixie face staring with concern. "Is everything all right, madam?"

"Quite all right. I just need to make a telephone call."

The telephone—more modern than the original

candlestick version—with a cradle receiver that hung on two brass clips jutting from a sturdy base, was on the desk of Ginger's study. Formerly the domain of her late father, Ginger had kept the masculine decor of dark wood and dark shades of green and purple paint and wallpaper. A bookcase lined one wall and a stone fireplace another. A framed painting of a young George Hartigan hung where Ginger, when seated in her new leather office chair, could gaze upon it fondly.

She cradled the receiver between her ear and shoulder and dialled Scotland Yard. When the operator connected her, she asked for Basil.

"This is Constable Braxton, Mrs. Reed. The chief inspector is in the middle of an interview."

Ginger wagered a guess. "Did you find Miss Darby?"

After a slight hesitation, Constable Braxton answered, "We did, madam."

"Is she there now?"

A pause, then, "Yes, madam."

Hanging up, Ginger got to her feet. She didn't have time to do her hair or check her makeup. She'd left one of her many coats in the study earlier and grabbed it.

Once in the garage, Ginger pushed the starter button of the Crossley, listened for the roar of the motor, then backed out—her side mirror missing the edge of the door by an inch. Racing the vehicle down the back lane, she bumped over the rough edge and onto the main thoroughfare.

Ginger's mind returned to the last time she'd seen Lord Whitmore as he'd mingled with the gentlemen as if preferring their company to that of his wife. Unbidden, a song the band had played filled her head, and she sang aloud, "When the red, red robin, comes bob, bob, bobbin' along." How wonderful it would be if one could put a radio in a motorcar! Imagine that, listening to the BBC whilst driving in London. Music would make the traffic jams so much more tolerable.

Just as she drove around Trafalgar Square, she spotted Mr. Tipper, from the London News Agency, walking away from the Palace of Westminster. On the prowl for a story, Ginger concluded, or had he been tipped off about Lord Whitmore's demise and had been sniffing around the House of Lords?

When she strolled into the reception area of Scotland Yard, Constable Braxton sat behind the counter. She greeted the young man with a warm smile. "Good afternoon, Constable."

"Good afternoon, Mrs. Reed. How are you?"

"Very well, thank you."

"And your household?"

Ginger felt her lips twitch at the poor man's benign-sounding question. She knew the only member of her household he was asking about was Felicia, and a certain flirtatious encounter on the staircase with Mr. Fulton crossed her mind. She decided to sidestep the subtle probe.

"Everyone is well, if a little chilly. We miscalculated our need for coal at this time of year—" At least for a place the size of Hartigan House, but Ginger thought it would be tactless to say it aloud.

Constable Braxton commiserated. "Can't be helped with that dreadful unrest at the mines."

"Indeed," Ginger acknowledged. "I've heard the miners are refusing to work. Is Chief Inspector Reed in his office?"

"Ah—"

"No need to announce me. I know my way." Ginger waved her gloved fingers in the perplexed officer's direction and hurried along. She tapped on the open door of Basil's office before stepping inside.

Basil's head jerked up in surprise. He rose to his feet to greet her.

"Ginger? Is everything all right?"

They shared a short kiss in greeting, the door was open after all, and then Ginger calmed Basil's concerns with a smile. "Everything's fine. I'm just on my way to the office, and I thought I'd drop in to see if you've learned anything new. I understand from Constable Braxton that Miss Darby was located?"

Ginger smelled a hint of the perfume she'd noticed

at Miss Darby's flat, proof that the mistress had recently been in her husband's office and likely sitting in the very chair she herself now occupied. She noticed the wilted plant on the filing cabinet and wondered if the strength of the woman's scent had killed it. Basil saw her looking at it.

"That was a thank you gift from my last case. Unfortunately, neither I nor any of the officers here have green fingers."

"You could've brought it home," Ginger said, though she also didn't have green fingers, or as they'd say in Boston, a green thumb. However, Clement would've made the poor plant flourish.

"It slipped my mind," Basil said, then answered her first question. "Yes, Miss Darby was located. She claims to have spent a couple of hours in a hair salon."

"You don't believe her?"

His lip pulled up as if he failed to believe getting one's hair done could be measured in a matter of hours. "It's a rather long time."

"What did she claim to have done?"

Basil wrinkled his brow as if this question were the last one he'd think Ginger would ask. "Er, cut, colour, and waves?"

"Oh, that most definitely would take a couple of hours. Though she could've killed Lord Whitmore before she left."

"That's what I thought, but I've just heard from the pathologist, and he's suggesting that the time of death was between ten and twelve. Mr. Savage claims that Miss Darby left before that time. Miss Darby's hair appointment was for ten this morning—Sergeant Scott confirmed it—so it would seem likely that she would've left her flat before then. However, it's a very close timetable."

Ginger agreed with that assessment. She asked, "Was Miss Darby distraught?"

Basil shrugged a shoulder. "She was rather, though it's hard to know for sure her sincerity. However, I can't come up with a motive as to why Miss Darby would go to such drastic measures to rid herself of a man, especially one of means and social standing. Surely, she could've just put an end to the assignations."

"What about Lady Whitmore?"

"The widow's emotions were more complicated. She and Lord Whitmore lived rather separate lives, and she couldn't easily name his regular friends or places he liked to frequent."

Ginger tapped the tip of her nose with a perfectly polished fingernail. "Yet, she made a stop at the bank just to see him. She must've had her suspicions."

"She had a rather full schedule on Saturday, and claimed to have stayed in Sunday morning before ringing the police," Basil added with a tilt of his chin.

"She claims to have remained at home all this morning as well."

"So, she could've popped up to Miss Darby's flat and found her husband in the bathtub."

"Yes, but it begs the question of how she would know which flat belonged to Miss Darby and how she'd learned of their ongoing liaison?"

"That's not so difficult." In jest, Ginger tipped the brim of her hat down and tugged up her coat collar. "One simply follows from a distance."

A look of astonishment flashed behind Basil's eyes, and Ginger chuckled as she readjusted her hat and collar.

"Not that I've followed you, love. But Lady Whitmore could have, on an earlier occasion, watched the door to the bank from the coffee lounge across the street and then followed him into Miss Darby's building. It's not like there's a doorman to check in with and not everyone bothers to lock their doors all the time."

"Yes, but unless we can capture fingerprints or find a witness who's seen her inside that building, we have no proof."

Ginger sighed. "We're back to square one, aren't we?"

Basil pushed away from his desk. "Let's pop into the House of Lords, then track down Mr. Poole, shall we? I take it you drove?"

"I did."

"Let's take my Austin."

Ginger held in a grin. Basil hadn't been shy about telling her he didn't enjoy her style of driving. She accepted his hand as he offered to help her out of her chair.

"Oh, I almost forgot," she said. "I had a dream about Miss Darby."

"Indeed?"

"About her wardrobe, and it reminded me of something I saw there. It's probably not important, but I remember seeing a *sarafan* amongst the other items."

"A sarafan?"

"Scout asked me about communist propaganda whilst on our ride. It seems Mr. Fulton likes to discuss social issues, and it reminded me that I saw a sarafan in Miss Darby's wardrobe."

"Please do educate me, love. What is a sarafan?"

"It's a Russian traditional folk costume. It looked authentic to me. I think our Miss Darby may have been to Russia."

## 10

he Palace of Westminster—or as many referred to it, the Houses of Parliament— where the House of Lords resided, was only a short jaunt west of Scotland Yard along Victoria Embankment. Ginger wasn't sure what they quite hoped to accomplish when they stepped out of Basil's motorcar, since it wasn't likely that the members were congregating around the palace waiting to be interviewed, and they couldn't just traipse through without permission.

Ginger studied Basil's expression for clues to his intention. The corner of his mouth tugged up. "Let me know if you recognise anyone."

Ginger scanned the figures going to and from the palace doors, mostly men, in search of a lord she might know in passing. Though recently a lady herself,

Ginger hadn't resided in London all that long, and though she prided herself on her social finesse, she hadn't encountered all of London's polite society.

The palace itself was an imposing structure with sharp edges, turrets, and the iconic Big Ben tower. The neo-Gothic masterpiece, spread out royally along the glistening Thames, glowed as if golden.

Finding a lord in the mix was rather like the proverbial needle in the haystack.

Ginger cast a sideways glance at her husband. Basil, a long-time resident of London, and the son of an "Honourable", wasn't without his connections. Together, with necks craned, they searched for a familiar face, and Ginger was almost ready to give up when she saw someone she knew.

"There's Lord Hastings!"

They picked up their pace along the pavement, and when they were at an acceptable distance behind the lord, Ginger called out. "Lord Hastings."

On hearing his name, the gentleman came to an abrupt stop. Turning to face them, the loose flesh on his cheeks tightened into a smile when his deep-set eyes landed on Ginger.

"Lady Gold?"

"It's Mrs. Reed now, Lord Hastings." She motioned to Basil. "This is my husband, Chief Inspector Reed."

Lord Hastings extended his hand to Basil. "How do you do?"

"Quite well, sir," Basil returned with a firm hand-shake. "And you?"

"Very well, indeed." He stared back at Ginger with a look of expectancy. "Fancy meeting you here."

Their voices were temporarily drowned out by the honking from a passing bus followed by the tin ringing of bells from cyclists zooming unapologetically past slower-moving pedestrians.

"Yes, well," Ginger began once she was assured of their physical safety. "I must confess, we've called out to you because Basil is looking into the death of Lord Whitmore."

Lord Hastings' jowls grew slack. "Whitmore's dead? Are you sure?"

"Quite," Basil said. "News of the sad event hasn't been relayed to the papers yet."

The lord worked his thin lips. "I heard he was missing, but I thought he'd just—"

"Just?" Basil prompted.

"Not to speak ill of the dead, but he had wandering eyes and often took short trips of a certain nature away from home."

"Was Lord Whitmore at odds with any of the members of the House?" Ginger asked.

Lord Hastings shrugged thick shoulders. "No, I

can't say that he was. Whitmore was an amiable fellow and mostly kept to himself. Cast his vote when necessary, but other than that, he didn't spend a lot of time in the Members' Dining Room like many of us."

One thing Ginger had learned whilst working for the British secret service, was that one was to keep one's relationships shallow and therefore dispensable. Which was why, now that she had Basil and Scout in her life, she could never re-engage with the agency.

"Can you think of anyone who might've wished Lord Whitmore harm?" she asked.

"I honestly can't," Lord Hastings said. "But if I hear of anything I believe might be of interest to the police, I'll be sure to contact you."

Basil shook the gentleman's hand again. "I'd be much obliged."

Ginger and Basil darted through a jungle of circling black, high-top motor vehicles, and Ginger felt strangely exhilarated and relieved that they had made it back to Basil's Austin in one piece.

She glanced at Basil, who fiddled with the starter button. "The Poole residence?"

Basil nodded. "I had Braxton track down an address in Farringdon."

The drive to the Pooles' townhouse was uneventful. Basil is so terribly sensible, Ginger mused, now evident by the careful and studious way he drove.

Banking hours meant that Mr. Poole should be home from work at this later hour of the afternoon, assuming he came here directly.

A lady with small black eyes lodged in a doughy face answered the door and stared at Ginger and Basil.

"Are you Mrs. Poole?"

The timid lady nodded.

"I'm Chief Inspector Reed, and this is my consultant, Lady Gold." Ginger and Basil had agreed to use her former title when she officially joined him on his investigations, as it sounded more professional than calling her his wife.

Ginger thrust out a gloved hand. "Of Lady Gold Investigations."

Mrs. Poole limply shook her hand.

"We have a few questions to ask Mr. Poole about a former manager. Is he home?"

Mrs. Poole waved them inside and closed the door behind them.

"He's in the living room listening to the wireless," Mrs. Poole said softly. "I'm not a fan of the instrument myself. Fills the house with noise, and I can't get the man to say one word to me when it's on."

The townhouse, properly clean and tastefully decorated, carried the scent of roast duck through the air. Mr. Poole proved slightly hard of hearing as the programme was a trifle loud. He startled when he saw them standing in the doorway, quickly turned the volume knob down, and jumped to his feet. "My, this is a surprise!"

"We do apologise for disturbing your programme," Basil said, "I'm afraid I have bad news regarding Lord Whitmore."

Mr. Poole sobered. "Oh dear me, where are my manners. Please have a seat."

As Ginger and Basil settled on the settee, Mr. Poole turned to his wife. "Perhaps a bit of tea, love?"

Basil interrupted. "Tea isn't necessary, not on our behalf. We shan't be long."

Mrs. Poole left the room anyway. Mr. Poole returned to his armchair, a favourite by the looks of the worn-out armrests, and leaned in with an earnest expression on his face. "What happened to His Lordship?"

Basil removed a short pencil and small notepad from his suit pocket. "Lord Whitmore's body was found this morning. I'm afraid I'm not at liberty to discuss the details at this point."

The banker's forehead creased high onto his bald head. "I'm very sorry to hear it. How can I help you?"

"How long had Lord Whitmore been occupying a position at your bank?"

"A year and a half, and not to be disrespectful, I couldn't tell you exactly what it was that he did."

Ginger raised a thin brow. "Duties belonging to a bank manager, I suspect?"

Mr. Poole's gaze moved from Ginger's face.

"Yes, one would think so, but apparently Lord Whitmore had been given whatever leeway he desired."

"Why do you suppose that was?" Basil asked.

"I have no idea. It's frightfully out of the ordinary." Mr. Poole sniffed. "It's not as if he needed money. He simply had too much time on his hands. Someone pulled strings because he was a *Lord*. I doubted that he would be satisfied with the work for long. Quite honestly, I was waiting for him to grow restless and leave the position. Make it available for someone else."

Like Mr. Poole? Ginger thought. Would this middle-class banker kill for a promotion? Ginger and Basil shared a look.

"Steady on," Mr. Poole said, belatedly making the connection himself. "You never said how Lord Whitmore died. I assumed a heart attack or something. Don't tell me he was murdered?"

"I'm afraid so, Mr. Poole," Basil said. "Can you tell me your whereabouts this morning?"

"You don't think that I—"

"It's just a matter of form," Basil said. "I assure you."

"I was at the bank the whole time. Unlike, well . . .

er . . . some, I keep my hours and do my job. You can ask anyone there. I was in the building from eight o'clock until noon."

"Are you privy to the state of Lord Whitmore's finances?" Basil asked.

Mr. Poole's shoulders relaxed as the subject moved off himself.

"I'm aware that Lord Whitmore owned property, and surely, he had other investments. I can only assume by his lifestyle that he had enough to live comfortably."

He sniffed again. "A banker's salary wouldn't have altered his that much, and another worthy man in a lesser situation would've been happy to have that position."

"I suppose that position is available now," Ginger said.

Mr. Poole stared back solemnly. "I suppose it is."

"It's rumoured that you were coveting Lord Whitmore's position." It was a solid motive, Ginger thought. Mr. Poole would look like a reasonable and desirable replacement, especially if the word on how the lord had died got out.

"I know what you're thinking, Mrs. Reed," Mr. Poole said. "But I'm not your man."

. . .

As THEY RETURNED to the motorcar, Ginger mentioned her suspicions about Mr. Poole.

"He's obviously quite disgruntled at what he considers an injustice. I can see his point. Why should Lord Whitmore get a coveted position at the bank simply because of his station in life? These are precisely the arguments presented by the Communist Party of Great Britain."

"Perhaps Lord Whitmore had jumped the queue because of his title, but you don't really believe communism is the answer?"

"Of course not. I'm simply stating that I understand why those who live without certain privileges would feel so strongly."

"Strongly enough to take matters into their own hands and commit murder?"

"It's been done before."

Once they were both seated in the motorcar, Basil announced his next stop.

"I'm going to drop in at the Yard's mortuary to see Dr. Wood. Would you like to join me, or shall I deliver you somewhere else first?"

"Oh, I most definitely would like to come along." Ginger was acquainted with Dr. Wood because her good friend Haley Higgins, who now lived in Boston, had worked alongside the pathologist on a previous case.

At the mortuary, they found Dr. Wood dressed in a white lab coat and holding a bloody scalpel in his hand. He looked up through round spectacles when Ginger and Basil entered the mortuary.

"Sorry to interrupt, Doctor," Basil said. "I'm hoping you have some new information for me."

Ginger could feel Basil's growing tension. A lord had been viciously murdered, and they had no good leads. The more time that went by without one, the higher the odds were that the case wouldn't be solved.

The body of Lord Whitmore was on the table, and Dr. Wood pulled the sheet over the freshly sewn-up Y incision. A tray of organs lay on a table.

"I was just examining the stomach contents," Dr. Wood said. "Lord Whitmore had consumed a breakfast of scrambled eggs and toast, and a good amount of tea. Apart from a few extra pounds, he seemed to be in relatively good shape and would've enjoyed several more years.

He stared over his spectacles. "Cause of death is what you assumed. He was electrocuted. I'm afraid I don't have more than that to offer."

"Can you confirm the time of death?" Ginger asked.

"No more than what I relayed to the chief inspector earlier. In my estimation, death occurred between ten a.m. and twelve noon."

According to Mr. Savage, Miss Darby had left her flat at fifteen minutes to ten. It was a close call when it came to an alibi, but a good solicitor would throw the theory of Miss Darby's involvement out of court if Ginger and Basil couldn't find more evidence against her.

"Thank you," Basil said. "Please let me know if anything of importance comes from the laboratory testing."

"Of course, Chief Inspector."

Ginger and Basil returned to Basil's office. Ginger closed the door, then wrapped her arms around her husband's neck. "I'm going to call in at my office before heading home."

Basil kissed her on the lips. "I'll meet you there in time for dinner."

One more kiss, then Ginger reluctantly pulled away. "See you there, love."

## 11

*G*inger liked to keep her work and private life separate and purposely kept her home telephone number and address off her Lady Gold Investigations business cards. It meant that someone needed to stay in the office to answer the telephone or make appointments for Ginger with clients who might walk in off the streets. That person was usually Felicia, but it was still Ginger's responsibility to call in for messages.

Though it was out of her way, Ginger headed back to Fleet Street before dropping in at the office. The newspaper stand on the corner reminded her of Mr. Tipper, the journalist she'd spotted coming out of Miss Darby's building Sunday, and then earlier that day around the Houses of Parliament. Ginger didn't count him as a suspect, at least she hadn't since she couldn't think of a reasonable motive for a newspaperman to want to kill Lord Whitmore, but he could be a witness. It was certainly worth stopping at the London News Agency to speak to the man.

A few blasts of angry honking later, and Ginger pulled her motorcar to a stop in front of the three-storey red-brick building and went inside.

"I'd like to speak to Mr. Tipper," Ginger announced to the unenthusiastic-looking receptionist, "if he's in." The nameplate on the desk said Miss Ryerson. Ginger smiled and added, "Miss Ryerson."

Miss Ryerson pushed a pair of round wire-rimmed spectacles along the bridge of a narrow nose. "Whom shall I say is calling?"

"Tell him it's Lady Gold from Lady Gold Investigations."

Miss Ryerson shot her a look of interest, then her gaze went blank as she picked up the internal telephone. Ginger suspected there wasn't much the woman hadn't seen or heard.

"Please have a seat, Lady Gold," Miss Ryerson said as she removed her headset. "He'll be with you in a moment."

Mr. Tipper must've been intrigued at the prospect of Ginger waiting as he materialised within minutes.

"Ah, the famed Lady Gold," he said, his smile broad and his eyes twinkling. He reached out a hand

and shook hers warmly. "Such an honour to finally meet you face to face."

His smile lingered in his chocolate-brown eyes, and though not classically handsome, he radiated charm.

"Please follow me." His eyes darted to Miss Ryerson, who was quite diplomatically keeping her eyes averted, but Ginger didn't doubt she took in every nuance.

"Thank you," Ginger said. "I only need a moment of your time."

Much like every other newsroom Ginger had been to, a buzz of sound filtered through the building: a mix of typewriter keys clicking, telephones ringing, low voices carrying on one-sided conversations, and telegram machines growling. Mr. Tipper opened the door to a small interview room that smelled of stale air and cigarette smoke.

He pulled a wooden chair out for Ginger, and she thanked him. Taking the seat opposite, Mr. Tipper propped the elbows of his pin-striped suit on a scarred wooden table and leaned in eagerly. "Do you have a story for me, Lady Gold?"

Ginger blinked. "I'm not sure. I don't mean to mislead you, Mr. Tipper. I've come to ask you a question that is quite possibly none of my business."

Mr. Tipper smirked. "Exactly the kind of questions I like. Ask away."

"I saw you leave a residential building on Sunday, just down the street from here, number twenty-one. Would you mind telling me what you were doing there?"

Mr. Tipper deflated like a balloon. "You're right. It's not your business."

"I'm hoping you'll humour me, anyway, Mr. Tipper."

"What's in it for me?"

"I'm consulting on a murder case. Your cooperation will look good for you, and the press in general."

"Murder, you say? Might I ask who's died?"

"I'm afraid I'm not at liberty to say at the moment."

"What does that have to do with m—" Leo Tipper blanched. "No, wait, it's not Gladys Darby, is it?"

"How do you know Miss Darby?"

He flushed with a look of mortification. "She's not . . . dead, is she?"

Ginger replied quickly, "No, she's not."

Mr. Tipper's relief was palpable. "Thank God."

"I'm going to assume you are acquainted with Miss Darby," Ginger said.

Mr. Tipper pulled at his collar. "In a manner of speaking."

"Was she home when you called in to see her on Sunday."

He grunted. "Home, but not alone, if you know what I mean."

"So, you're aware that Miss Darby had at least one gentleman friend other than you?"

"And if I was?"

"It would give you a motive, Mr. Tipper. Jealousy."

Mr. Tipper's jaw dropped. Ginger had the feeling the journalist wasn't often at a loss for words.

"Are you saying the fellow Gladys was entertaining is the victim?"

"Are you saying that you didn't kill the man?"

"Yes!" Mr. Tipper stabbed the table with a fountain pen, and Ginger now understood how the table had been damaged. "I'm not a killer, Lady Gold, I write stories about killers. And I want this story. Who was the victim?"

Ginger shifted off the uncomfortable chair and rose to her feet. "I'm afraid that information can't come from me. However, I think you'll agree I've given you enough to go on." Reaching into her handbag, Ginger retrieved a business card and held it out to Mr. Tipper. "If you find anything that may be of interest to me in my quest to solve this murder, please contact me."

Mr. Tipper's titillating smile returned. "Certainly, milady. I'd be pleased to share trade secrets with you."

Ginger drove on to Watson Street and was happy

to see that the door to Lady Gold Investigations was unlocked, which meant Felicia was on the premises.

"Oh, Ginger," Felicia said when she saw her. "We have a guest."

Ginger recognised the man sitting in one of the chairs in front of her desk: her second meeting with a journalist in so many hours. How unusual.

"Hello, Mr. Brown," she said as she removed her coat and hung it on the rack. "How nice to see you. I've wanted to thank you for the lovely story you wrote about my party and the adoption of my son."

"It was my pleasure, Mrs. Reed." Mr. Brown fiddled with a well-chewed pencil. "But I heard about a death in the peerage through the grapevine. I confess I'm hurt that you haven't rung me about the story."

Ginger swallowed back the guilt she felt at having just recently given Mr. Tipper a lead.

"It's been a busy day, and I haven't been given clearance to ring the press. You know you'd be my first call if I had."

Mr. Brown flicked a palm. "Water under the bridge." With a quick nibble on his pencil, the journalist continued, "Readers are tired of hearing about labour unrest, bolshie unrest, and idle bomb threats. A good juicy murder is what they need."

"What makes you think Lord Whitmore's death was a murder?"

"Well, first, I didn't know it was Lord Whitmore, so thank you for that."

Ginger scowled. She was losing her touch. With each year that passed from her work with the British secret service during the war, the sloppier she seemed to get. She'd never let intelligence information escape her lips like that before, although, it wasn't as if word wasn't about to get out. Blake Brown knew about the death. Lady Whitmore was a notorious gossip, and even though the scandal had involved the lady herself, she was unlikely to keep the news a secret.

Blake Brown smirked in response. "And to answer your second question, you wouldn't be involved if it weren't a murder. Or at least your husband wouldn't be."

"You follow my husband's cases?"

"Of course."

Felicia stared at Ginger with a wounded look. "Is it true? Lord Whitmore has been murdered? Why am I always the last to know?"

"You're not always the last to know, love," Ginger said kindly, "and now you both know. Lord Whitmore was murdered sometime before noon yesterday. I really can't say how he died, only that there are several people of interest." She stared pointedly at Mr. Brown. "I'm afraid I can't give you more than that."

Mr. Brown nodded his head like a toy dog with a

spring neck. "Very well. But do ring me the moment the brass says you can." He shuffled to his feet and tipped his hat. "Good day, ladies."

Ginger watched Mr. Brown leave and listened for the sound of the bell chime above the door to fade away.

"You must tell me everything!" Felicia said excitedly. "I've hit a wall with my story. Perhaps a real-life crime will inspire me."

"I'm afraid I can't say anything yet."

Felicia let out an exasperated breath. "Fine. I'll just read about it in the papers like everyone else. One would think having two detectives in one's family would be an advantage."

Ginger laughed. "Sorry to disappoint you, love."

Felicia stretched out her arms. "I've done enough writing today anyway, and now my back is killing me. Are you going home soon?"

Ginger stared at the pile of unopened mail. She would rather leave it until later, but then it would just create more work for later.

"I'm going to stay for a while," she said.

Felicia sighed dramatically then grabbed her coat. "I'll take the tube. It's faster than driving anyway. Brian doesn't mind waiting."

Ginger sliced open an envelope with a brass letter

opener and stopped halfway. "Constable Braxton? I thought you were sweet on Mr. Fulton."

"They're both lovely, aren't they?"

Ginger let the half-opened envelope drop to the desk. "Felicia! It's very unladylike to play with a gentleman's feelings. You're leading one or the other on, or heaven forbid both. It's unkind and a –"

"What would the neighbours think? You sound like Grandmama."

"Ambrosia isn't always wrong, Felicia. You could learn a thing or two from your elders. Loyalty, devotion, and there's something to be said about respectability."

Felicia snorted. "Are you worried about my reputation or yours?"

Ginger sighed. The last thing she wanted was a relational rift with Felicia. "Does either gentleman know about the other?"

Felicia lifted a shoulder, staying silent.

"I'm just saying that maybe you should choose one and let the other be. A life of deception is no life at all."

"Fine!" Felicia grabbed her coat and handbag. "I promise to choose one and break the heart of the other." She flicked her wrist and glanced at her watch. "I want to catch the next train."

The door had just snapped shut behind Felicia when Ginger had a change of heart about working late.

She was too fatigued to give the correspondence its due attention, and now she felt a little heartsick over her conversation with Felicia. Perhaps she'd been a little heavy-handed with her former sister-in-law.

"Felicia, wait!" Ginger slipped on her coat and searched for her office keys. She was sure she'd dropped them in there, but then her fingers brushed against something in her pocket. She removed a small piece of folded paper, good quality paper by the feel of it. Opening it, Ginger stared at the typed letters, and her blood cooled.

Code. She recognised the style from the war, and even more recently from a case involving a body found at Feathers & Flair.

Lord Whitmore had been involved in that case as well. Ginger couldn't accept the coincidence.

What could this mean? How had this note got into her coat?

Then she remembered. The last time she'd worn this powder-blue, double-button coat, was the day she'd run into Lord Whitmore on Fleet Street. She'd thought the run-in had been accidental, but perhaps he'd seen her coming.

What was the coded message, and why had he given it to her?

Ginger pushed the note back into her pocket and grabbed her keys from her other pocket, but before she could leave, the bell above the door rang. Had her sister-in-law returned? Perhaps she also felt bad about how their conversation had ended.

"Felicia?"

"Sorry, dear," a male voice said. "It's me."

Ginger froze to the spot.

"Captain Smithwick?"

Captain Francis Smithwick hadn't lost his stern posture or stiff upper lip, though his temples had greyed since Ginger had last seen him, and the wrinkles around his eyes had grown more pronounced. It hadn't been that long since the captain had last interrupted her life, trifling with Felicia's heart to manipulate her, but deceitful living had a way of aging a person. Wearing his military uniform, he carried his cap in his hand and returned Ginger's look of bewilderment with one of authority. If there was one person in the world whom Ginger loathed, it was this man.

Ginger dispensed with pleasantries. "What are you doing here?"

Captain Smithwick's lips twitched. "Why, dear, I'm here to see you."

Ginger strapped her handbag over her shoulder. "I'm afraid I was just leaving. You'll have to call and make an appointment." Which she'd be sure to ignore.

"I only need a moment of your time. I promise."

Ginger sighed, then relented. Captain Smithwick

was the kind of man who didn't give up until he got what he wanted. She'd save time if she just let him deliver his message. Motioning to one of the client chairs, she said, "Have a seat." She returned to her own, leaving her coat on as a signal this meeting would be short.

"I'm here on behalf of His Majesty."

*Oh mercy.* Was he about to try to recruit her again? The last time he'd attempted that, Felicia had been hurt terribly. Thank goodness she'd left the office when she had.

"I really don't—"

"Before you decline and disappoint the King, please allow me to state my case."

Ginger thought about the coded note in her coat pocket. Perhaps Lord Whitmore had been killed because of something he'd been working on with the secret service? It couldn't be yet another coincidence that Captain Smithwick had appeared so soon afterwards, could it? Whatever the threat was, and if Captain Smithwick was involved, it was most assuredly a threat, it was in London, not on Continental shores. This was close to home.

Ginger pursed her lips and blew a defeated breath.

"I'm listening."

## 12

"*A*re you all right, love?"

Ginger's gaze touched Basil, who stared over his morning coffee with a look of tenderness in his hazel eyes. It was his eyes that had attracted Ginger when she'd first glimpsed him on their shared journey from Boston to Liverpool on the SS *Rosa*. Warm and intelligent with enough lines fanning from the corners to confirm life experience, they were a bright contrast to his dark hair which was greying at the temples. In retrospect, she was sure it had been love at first sight, though they were both too mature and truthfully, too wounded to admit it at the time.

The SS *Rosa* had also brought Scout into her life. She was grateful for the vessel and the excursion that had brought her to London.

"Ginger?"

Ginger snapped out of her reverie. "Oh, yes. Quite fine."

"You look tired. Did you not sleep well?"

"I didn't for some reason." Ginger, purposely vague, was sure of the reason. His name was Captain Smithwick and his proposal had had her tossing and turning all night. Accepting would mean taking on a case that she'd have to keep from Basil. It wasn't like she shared the details of all the cases that came through the doors of Lady Gold Investigations, but she didn't have to keep them top secret either.

She smiled for Basil's benefit and added, "I'm sure I'll get a second wind soon."

With breakfast, the morning room was always a revolving door; everyone came in as they willed, quite aware that Mrs. Beasley's breakfast buffet was waiting on the sideboard. Ambrosia, an early riser, had been and gone; Scout, finishing his egg, ran off to brush his teeth and get ready for his schooling with Mr. Fulton; and Felicia had yet to appear.

Ginger took a bite of her buttered toast then said, "I suppose you'll be continuing your investigation into Lord Whitmore's death?" It sounded like a benign question, and under normal circumstances, it would've been. Her toast suddenly felt dry in her mouth. She hated the feeling of being on a different side of things from her husband. She could say no to Smithwick. Perhaps that would be best.

"Yes, though I'm not sure what else to do that I haven't already done. Whoever is responsible for this has covered up his steps well. From all accounts, Lord Whitmore lived a fairly quiet life."

It was at times like this when Ginger particularly hated her oath to the Official Secrets Act. If she could speak freely, she'd tell Basil all she knew about Lord Whitmore, that the man's life was anything but placid, and that she had a coded message.

Instead, she sipped her tea.

"How about you, love?" Basil asked. "What are your plans for the day?"

Basil asked the question every morning, and most mornings, her answer was similar: see to Scout, take care of orders and correspondence for Feathers & Flair from her study at Hartigan House before driving to Regent Street to oversee the staff and happenings at the shop. From there, she'd meet up with Felicia at the office of Lady Gold Investigations. Should she be on a case, the order of those events could naturally be swapped.

"I think I'll stay close to home today. I can manage my work from the study."

The paper was delivered by Pippins, and the headlines, written in bold letters, could be read clearly across the room.

GENERAL STRIKE - TRADES UNION CONGRESS SUPPORTING MINERS

"Oh mercy," Ginger said.

She and Basil perused the news story together. Almost two million people had gone on strike at one minute to midnight.

Basil pinched his lips. "All the unions in England on strike at once will mean chaos."

Pippins returned with a stern expression on his face. Ginger felt a twinge of alarm, as old Pips rarely showed negative emotions.

"What is it, Pips?" she asked.

"I've just been listening to the wireless in the kitchen, madam. A special report broke the musical programme. A bomb has gone off on Fleet Street."

Basil sprang to his feet and raced out of the room. Ginger followed him, well aware he was heading for her study to use the telephone.

He had already dialled the operator when Ginger stepped in after him. "Connect me to Scotland Yard."

After a string of grunts accompanied by persistent frowning, Basil hung up. "No casualties, thankfully."

"Has anyone admitted responsibility?" Ginger asked.

"Not yet." Basil took Ginger's hand and kissed her

head. "I'm going to the Yard. I expect the streets to be crowded, so it might take a while."

Ginger understood Basil's need to do something and waved him off.

Encountering Felicia in the corridor, Ginger greeted her with a careful, "Good morning."

"I know, I slept in," Felicia said, her face newly painted and her eyes bright, "but I'm ready to go whenever you are." It seemed their harsh words the evening before were forgotten. Felicia's inability to hold a grudge was one of the many things Ginger loved about her.

"I'm going to work from home this morning," Ginger said. "You don't mind taking a taxicab to the office?"

"Oh," Felicia replied airily, "if I must. I'm nearing the end of my book, so I'm quite excited to get working on it. I think I dreamt of the answer to my story dilemma. I'll just have a bite to eat and be off."

"Don't forget to follow up on our last client."

"I expect news of his lost cousin to come in the post this afternoon."

"Perfect." Ginger held Felicia's gaze. "And be vigilant. There was news of a bombing this morning."

Felicia's mouth dropped open.

"A small explosion, no injuries. Just be careful."

"I shall."

Ginger returned to her study and tackled the post piled on her desk. She reviewed the fashion catalogues and magazines coming from Paris, particularly enjoying the French language ones as it kept the language sharp in her mind. It reminded her of Captain Smithwick's request, his bold solicitation. Outlandish, and yet much in line with how the secret service worked.

However, there must be someone else up to the task.

Ginger telephoned her shop manager, Madame Roux, who assured her that business was brisk and under control. New bolts of fabric were due to arrive in the next day or so, and Madame Roux promised to ring her the minute they did.

The door pushed open, and when she didn't see the face of Pippins or Lizzie or any other human, Ginger's gaze dropped lower to the ground.

"Hello, Bossy. Are Mr. Fulton's lessons boring you?"

Boss trotted to Ginger, his nails tip-tapping on the wooden floors, and she reached down to pat him on the head.

"You've come to help me make up my mind, haven't you? I know, I can't be an ostrich about it, can

I? If it's bad news, it's bad news whether I understand the message or not."

Boss cocked his head, nudged her calf with his wet nose as if to say "Get on with it". He then found his bed near the fireplace, though, with the few coals in the grate growing black, there wasn't exactly a lot of heat emanating from it.

The note was in her skirt pocket. After a deep sigh, she removed the folded scrap of paper.

Code.

A shiver slid down her spine.

EcQllqZdQor1

It was a literary Pandora's Box. Open at one's peril.

Ginger trembled and folded her arms as if to ward off a chill, but her physical response had nothing to do with the temperature of the room.

"We've done this once before, Bossy, remember? Shall we try the same trick?"

Ginger placed her fingers on the home row of her Underwood typewriter, then let her fingers drop one row. She typed out the coded message as if her index fingers were still on F and J.

"A garbled mess, Boss."

She tried a row above the home keys, which disappointed again, and then the row of numbers which performed as she expected. No sense whatsoever.

She wrinkled her nose. "It was too much to expect the same methodology, I suppose."

Pippins appeared after a tap on the door, and she expected that he'd arrived with the offer of tea, which she'd have gladly accepted, but his announcement was something else rather unexpected.

"You have a visitor, madam."

"Oh?" Ginger couldn't think who it might be. It was rare that someone called on her without prior arrangement, and she was strict about operating Lady Gold Investigations cases from the office and not her private house. "Who is it, Pips?"

"A Captain Smithwick, madam. He says he's an old acquaintance."

Ginger felt the warmth of anger and disdain rise. Pippins, always so in tune with Ginger's psyche, said, "Shall I turn him away, madam?"

Ginger was strongly tempted to say yes, but Captain Smithwick wasn't the sort to be put off. She wouldn't put it past him to push Pippins aside and march about the place until he found her.

"No. You can show him to the sitting room."

"Shall I arrange for tea?"

"That won't be necessary." Ginger didn't want to give Captain Smithwick any reason to stay longer than he had to.

# 13

*G*inger checked the time on her watch and waited a full ten minutes before entering the sitting room. Captain Smithwick rose to his feet, a smirk on his face.

"I suppose I deserved a bit of tardiness, having come without an invitation."

"You know I don't want you in my house."

Captain Smithwick lowered himself back into his chair, crossed his legs, and produced a silver cigarette case.

"Do you mind if I smoke?"

"I do, rather."

With a snort, Captain Smithwick returned the case to his pocket. His gaze roved down Ginger's body, and she quickly sat in the opposite chair.

"You're looking lovely, as usual," he said.

"Please, just get on with it."

"All business, then? Very well." The captain glanced about the room to ensure they were alone. "It's quite safe to speak freely here?"

"No one is listening in on us, at least that I'm aware of," Ginger said. "Unless you've put someone up to it."

"I'm not about to infringe on your privacy, Mrs. Reed."

Ginger didn't doubt for one minute that the captain would do that very thing, should he feel the Crown and national security found it necessary. She held her tongue.

"What I'm about to tell you is in the strictest confidence."

"Of course. I'd expect nothing else."

Captain Smithwick dragged his chair closer, then leaned in. "There is a communist cell in London. Our own Lord Whitmore was closing in, but, alas—"

Ginger leaned in. "Is that why he was killed?" Ginger's imagination began to churn. "Did he suspect his life was in danger?" Was that why he had given her the coded message?

"Unfortunately, Lord Whitmore's intelligence gathering was becoming suspect. His messages incoherent. His behaviour more irrational."

"Lady Whitmore mentioned that he'd become forgetful of late."

"We were about to pull him out of the field."

Ginger squinted. "You didn't have him, er, removed?" If the agency felt one of their own was about to endanger an operation, Ginger knew "removal" was an option.

Captain Smithwick smirked. "If we wanted to remove an agent, we'd do it in a way that didn't humiliate the family. You have to admit, his death is drawing the kind of attention the agency dislikes."

Ginger let out a breath. Lord Whitmore had died in service to his country, even if the situation appeared rather scandalous. "But you think this communist cell is responsible?"

"Quite undoubtedly."

"I'm not sure how you think I can be of service."

"We would very much like to know if Maxim Popov, a powerful member of the Bolshevik Revolutionary Party, leads it. If so, the situation is perilous, indeed. Popov is known to lie, manipulate, and wreak havoc to achieve his ends. We don't know a lot about him, except that he's a munitions expert."

"And, again, why do you need me?"

"It is known that there is an established cell in Paris, and intelligence has discovered that a certain member is coming to London to assist in recruiting members to the Communist Party. Our men are in position to create a . . . er . . . detour, you could say. To make room for you to step in. We believe you are the best we've got for this situation."

Ginger doubted that. She couldn't shake the feeling that Captain Smithwick only wanted to wield control over her life again. A twisted type of nostalgia.

"Where is this cell?" she asked.

Captain Smithwick actually looked abashed. "I must admit we don't know."

"How am I supposed to infiltrate it then?"

"Let's cross one bridge at a time, shall we? Besides, isn't investigating something you do? Finding things out for people?"

Ginger worked her lips. She couldn't disagree.

"Exactly," he replied. "So, are you game?"

There were many reasons Ginger should say no. Basil for one. Scout for another. But weren't they the very reasons she should do her bit to keep communism from infiltrating British society?

"Identifying the leader of this cell," she began, "how will it help you?"

"We would arrest him, take him off the streets. He's a huge influencer of the Communist Party of Great Britain. He can't be seen to be powerful. To cut off the head is to cut off the feet if you know what I mean."

"You want me to find the cell and then identify the members?"

"Correct. And this bloody strike business, though a nuisance, it's a distraction that could help you slip about undetected. Certainly, communications between Paris and London will be disrupted."

Ginger saw the logic in that reasoning. Captain Smithwick shifted in his chair, reached into his suit jacket, and removed an envelope. He extended an arm to Ginger, offering it to her.

"What is it?" she asked.

"Information on Margot Benac. It's an alias. We don't know her real name, only that she's a Russian spy working in Paris. She's the agent meant to come to London to support the cell here. My agents are at work to prevent that from happening. The strike and its consequences have overwhelmed wire services. We're confident the cell leaders here won't suspect an imposter."

Ginger arched a brow. "And you want me to impersonate her? This French woman?"

"It is your forte, is it not, *Mademoiselle LaFleur?*"

Ginger swallowed. She'd operated many missions in France during the war under the guise of Antoinette LaFleur. She'd revived Miss LaFleur once since then, to solve a tricky case, but she hadn't thought she'd ever do it again for the secret service.

In all honesty, it wasn't the secret service she resented—the organisation had its purpose—it was the man sitting across from her that made her seethe at a base level. He was responsible—in Ginger's mind—for her late husband's death. When the war ended, Ginger's fears had been confirmed: Daniel's life, and the lives of his company, had been quite needlessly lost.

Ginger removed a single sheet of paper from the envelope in her hands. On it was a grainy image of a woman's face and a few details such as height, weight, and hair colour. No name or background information.

Ginger glanced at the captain. "Not a lot here."

"We can't risk sensitive information getting into the wrong hands, but I thought it would be necessary for you to see what the lady you're to impersonate looks like."

"Definitely helpful."

"So, you'll do it?"

Co-operation with Captain Smithwick could lead her to the murderer of Lord Whitmore. And there was Scout to consider. Ginger didn't want her son living in a world where communism ruled. After a short breath, Ginger answered. "I'll give it a go, but under one condition."

"And that is . . . ?"

"Stay away from Felicia."

Captain Smithwick flicked a hand. "Look here. She was merely a pawn, as you know."

"You broke her heart, and I don't want to risk that again. Promise me you will do everything you can to prevent her from seeing you, including coming back here. If you need to contact me, do so by telephone. I'm either here, at my shop, or at my office."

Captain Smithwick stood. "Don't worry, Ginger. I know how to find you."

Ginger bristled at the familiar tone he took with her, using her first name. The captain donned his hat, bowed his chin, then turned towards the door. Ginger watched him go, already dreading their new alliance.

## 14

The next morning, Ginger arrived at Feathers & Flair to find Madame Roux spreading the morning paper across the counter with Dorothy and Emma flanking her on either side and reading over the shop manager's shoulder.

"The Trades Union Congress threatened to stall transport," Emma announced.

Dorothy jumped in, "And they've done it. I had to ride my bicycle to work due to the tube being closed."

Ginger had had a dashed time of it driving through clogged streets to get to the shop herself. It was too much to hope that the dispute would be resolved by the end of the day. Oh mercy, the drive home would be a nightmare.

"It'll be quiet in the shop," Madame Roux said.

"Our ladies won't risk stepping out with the threat of mayhem in the streets."

Ginger frowned. It had crossed her mind to close the shop, but she knew how her staff depended on their wages. "We can use the quiet to catch up on redesigning the show window and preparing for the summer rush."

"A new shipment of factory frocks arrived just before the strike," Dorothy said. "That'll keep me busy for a while."

Ginger nodded. The frocks had to be inventoried, carried upstairs, and displayed. Items with excessive wrinkles were ironed beforehand.

"And I have a lot of sewing projects to keep me busy," Emma said. "Mrs. Wilcox is quite adamant that I have her gown ready by Friday."

Madame Roux patted her sleek bob and then smoothed her skirt. "I can finally catch up with the books."

Satisfied that everyone was occupied, Ginger rang Hartigan House and left a message with Pippins for Felicia. "Tell her not to come to the office today. Public transport isn't running, and the roads are atrocious. All the taxicabs are busy as well. The streets are a veritable cacophony of motorcar horns."

Ginger spent time admiring the original designs Emma had sketched, reviewed the bolts of fabric on the shelves in the back room, and tried not to get in anyone's way. Her staff was more than capable and competent to run things without her hovering about, and for that, she was grateful. Life had a way of getting too busy as it was.

Her mind drifted to Captain Smithwick and his prophecy about the strike being a nuisance, but also a distraction. Though Ginger had agreed, in theory, to assist the captain, and by extension, the secret service, she was still at a loss as to how to go about it. How was one to infiltrate a group of people when one didn't know where they gathered?

The rhythmic clatter of Emma's sewing machine stopped and started as the seamstress expertly guided the fabric under the needle, her head bent low and gaze intense, while her foot worked the pedal.

Behind her, through the open door of the small office, Ginger could hear Madame Roux on the telephone. She spoke a blend of English and French, and Ginger presumed she was talking to a client in France.

English and French.

Ginger had an idea. "Emma?"

The machine slowed to a stop. "Yes, madam?"

"Please let Madame Roux know I'll be at my office if she needs me."

Emma ducked her head. "Yes, madam."

The office of Lady Gold Investigations was conveniently located around the corner from Feathers & Flair, and Ginger was thankful that she merely had to walk a few minutes to get there. Even in Mayfair, disgruntled drivers and pedestrians could be heard shouting at one another.

The air outside was warmer than in the lower level of the office, and Ginger mourned the lack of coal for the fireplace. She wrapped her spring coat around her waist more tightly.

She didn't need to stay long, only to test a new theory. She settled in at her desk, and produced the note with the code, flattening it out.

With her fingers over the keyboard of her typewriter, she once again lowered them one row, then typed.

Turning the roller, she removed the paper, the new message a new jumble of words.

Her time working in France had acquainted her well with the French keyboard which was designed differently from the English combination. For one, the number row at the top was accessed by first shifting as the letters with accents were more commonly used and were situated there. The Z and W were reversed as were the A and Q. The M was located beside the L in place of the colon and semi-colon key.

With a pencil, she replaced the English letters and

the numbers with the corresponding French keys and got: daorecallaw 1.

Ginger frowned at the nonsensical string of letters and numbers, then smiled. Her mind had automatically read it backwards: 1 Wallace Road.

She had an address.

Wallace Road was a short, dimly lit lane in a dense area around St. Clement Danes' Church near where Fleet Street becomes the Strand. Ginger took three times as long to drive there as she inched around slower vehicles and even, once or twice, drove onto the pavement—honking to get pedestrians to step aside. She settled with parking in an adjoining area, which, in retrospect, was preferred. The Crossley—a gorgeous vehicle with a shiny ivory exterior, white-rimmed tyres, polished chrome bumpers, an interior of luscious red leather, and a glossy teak dashboard—was easily recognised.

In this, her first reconnaissance mission, Ginger simply wanted to identify the entrance and see if anyone went in or came out.

The streets were a raucous zoo with people shouting, men dodging slow-moving vehicles, and motorcars being randomly abandoned as drivers got frustrated and decided to go about their business on foot. Horse traffic fared a bit better, and when the riders couldn't get their carts through, they simply unhitched and rode away through narrow openings and even on the pavements. When nature called, one large beast dropped its business on the street. Ginger wrinkled her nose and hoped a clean-up lad wasn't far behind.

Most of the foot traffic was men as most business was conducted by them. Ginger could count herself amongst fewer females, most of whom were well dressed in colourful spring frocks and hats adorned with feathers, ribbons, and fruit—the sort with money who could enjoy their leisure with shopping, much like the ladies who frequented Feathers & Flair.

A newsboy on the corner waved a paper like a flag and shouted, "Extra! Extra! Read all about the general strike!"

Even though the very same paper had been delivered to Hartigan House that morning, Ginger smiled at the lad and gave him sixpence.

"Thanks, madam."

The paper made a good shield, and though Ginger pushed her red locks up under her cloche hat as much as she could, she could still be easily recognised. She'd only just been featured in the social columns, and with a prominent dress shop in the city, she was bound to get recognised, eventually.

A teashop across the street from her mark made for a place to observe in relative comfort.

The person behind the counter apologised. "Sorry, madam, only day-olds. With this darn strike, we couldn't get the flour and lard delivered."

"I understand. I'll take a bun and a pot of tea."

"Jolly good. I'll bring it to your seat."

"I'll be over by the window."

Now that she was seated, the newspaper seemed somewhat superfluous, but she was glad to have given the news lad a bit of business.

The waitress came with her tea and bun, and Ginger was suddenly hungry. Rather famished. After the slight breakfast she'd had earlier that morning, it was to be expected. She added milk and sugar to the tea, and butter and jam to the bun, all with one eye turned on the obscure door across the street.

Police bells clanged loudly in the distance, and soon a troop of police officers poured onto the street to control the growing mob and trying, with little success, to move people along. Ginger recognised Constable Braxton in the mix and lifted her paper to hide her face, should he glance her way. This wasn't an area of London that Ginger regularly frequented, and she didn't want the constable to ask questions, or worse, tell Basil that he'd seen her there.

Over time, Constable Braxton moved further down

the street and out of Ginger's direct line of sight. So far, not a single person had gone through the door, and Ginger wondered if she'd misread the coded message. Perhaps it wasn't the address of the cell location, or maybe the cell had moved their meetings elsewhere. It would make sense if they believed that Lord Whitmore had sniffed them out.

Then a man approached the door. Of average size and height, he wore a loose-fitting suit. He glanced over his shoulder, but Ginger could not make out his face because of how low the brim of his trilby had been pulled down. The man unlocked the door then slipped inside.

Several more minutes passed without another person entering or leaving the premises. Ginger finished the last of her bun and tea then headed out onto the street. It was a good thing she'd grabbed her newspaper because she'd only just stepped onto the pavement when the door to 1 Wallace Road opened, and a blonde woman stepped out.

Ginger opened the paper and pretended to read as she watched the familiar form walk steadily away in the other direction.

"My, my," Ginger muttered. What was Miss Darby up to?

## 15

*B*asil was sympathetic to the strikers, but he couldn't help thinking it was all a deuced waste of time, not to mention how it upset life in the city. The mayhem certainly wasn't helping to solve the murder at hand.

Morris' round face crumpled in a stern expression of exasperation as he lumbered heavily into Basil's office and waved the *British Gazette*, the government newspaper, like a battered flag.

"Mr. Churchill, the Chancellor of the Exchequer says, 'I do not agree that the TUC have as much right as the Government to publish their side of the case and to exhort their followers to continue action'." The superintendent's bulbous eyes peered over the paper as if making sure Basil was listening before he continued with his recitation. "'It is a very much more difficult task to feed the nation than it is to wreck it.'"

"Indeed," Basil said. All his subordinates had been called into action as a "militia" of special constables.

Morris slapped the paper down on Basil's desk. "How am I to run the Yard when my men are busy trying to keep the strikers from wrecking the city?"

Basil opened his mouth, but Morris wasn't interested in a two-way conversation. "I've just got word that the blasted presses have shut down. What do the papers have to do with the miners? It's their job to report on all the ways the miners are breaking the law, not join in with them."

"I think that's the point, sir. The trade unions are supporting the miners for perceived injustices."

"Perceived is right. A deuced mess, if you ask me." Morris picked up the paper and folded it noisily. "How are you doing with the Whitmore case? I've got the Lord Mayor breathing down my neck, see? Apparently, Lady Whitmore and the Lord Mayor's wife are friendly."

"Yes, sir, well, I admit to having hit a bit of a dead end."

Morris stilled, his beady eyes turning to slits. "Already?"

"I've tracked every apparent lead, followed all the

usual protocol. There's surprisingly little one can find out about the man."

"There must be something, blast it! A man doesn't fall naked into a bathtub while holding a bloody radio."

Basil couldn't argue with his boss about that.

"Just do something, Reed."

"Yes, sir."

Morris left Basil's office, seemingly taking all the oxygen with him, and Basil had to take a moment to get his bearings. It was rare, but Basil did occasionally partake in cigarette smoking. He found a half-empty pack in a desk drawer along with matches and a dusty ashtray. He lit up, took a deep breath, then blew the plume of smoke towards the ceiling.

His notepad lay open on the desk in front of him, and he reviewed his notes. Of interest were the residential building caretaker, Mr. Savage; the mistress, Miss Darby; and the wife, Lady Whitmore. Also, potentially the manager at the bank, Mr. Poole, and anyone Lord Whitmore worked with.

Of all the people of note, he found Miss Darby, despite her apparent alibi, to be the most interesting. Women of ill-repute, whether they walked the streets or operated as sophisticated escorts, always knew things they didn't want anyone else to learn—unsavoury details about themselves and those they worked for. He also knew that women like Miss Darby were sealed tins, and even the hardiest tin opener would have the time of it, trying to open the contents.

Perhaps he should put a tail on her? Now that Lord Whitmore was gone, she must be in the market for another wealthy arm to hang on. If only all his men weren't tied up with this strike catastrophe.

Basil tapped the long ash that had formed on his cigarette as it sat on the ashtray, took another drag, then stubbed it out. He'd find Braxton—the young constable had a face the ladies liked—and if Miss Darby caught on to him following her, he might get her to talk to him anyway.

On his way out, Basil asked the lone clerk to what area of the city Braxton had been directed.

"Where Fleet Street becomes Ludgate Hill, sir."

Getting through the crowded street was arduous, and Basil regretted driving his Austin, but all the police vehicles had been in use. He stuck his head out of the window and shouted, "Police! Make way!"

Just ahead, a fistfight broke out, and Basil glimpsed a man in a police uniform blowing madly on his whistle. Basil pulled his Austin as close to the kerb as was possible and jumped out.

"Break it up, men!" Basil roared. "Break it up! In the name of the law!"

The bobby had his truncheon out, and as Basil approached, the rabble-rousers fled.

"Constable?" Basil said. The man faced him as he swiped at the blood leaking from his nose, and Basil couldn't believe his good fortune. "Braxton? I was just looking for you."

BASIL HAD BEEN WORRIED that they might have to get out and walk, but with enough determination and not a lot of patience, he managed to drive back to Hartigan House and parked the Austin in the garage in the back garden.

"I feel like I've kidnapped you," Basil said, opening his car door.

Braxton, who looked a little worse for wear, had a swollen nose and an abrasion on his cheek darkening into a bruise.

"You're certainly not on duty anymore," Basil said.

"It's quite all right, sir. I've nothing but leftover stew and a grumpy cat waiting for me at home."

"A hungry cat now."

"Ah, he's chubby enough. And there are always mice if he's that hungry. The window's open so he can come and go."

Basil hadn't even had a chance to tell Braxton why

he wanted him. All the mayhem on the streets had required Basil's full attention.

Clement greeted them and promised to look after Braxton while Basil searched for Ginger. Pippins waited in the back corridor, ready to receive Basil's coat and jacket. It amazed Basil how efficient the staff was, perpetually at the ready, and clearly communicating with one another.

"Thank you, Pippins,"

Pippins bowed his head. "Sir."

Female voices drifted from the sitting room, and Basil, fortifying himself, shouldered the double door and stepped inside. A quick perusal confirmed that the Dowager Lady Gold and Felicia were in a meeting that didn't include his wife. The two Gold ladies stared at him with expectation.

"Hello, Basil," Felicia said.

Though his instincts were to step rapidly out of the room, protocol dictated that he take a few minutes to engage in polite conversation. He stepped inside but didn't go as far as to take a seat.

"Hello, ladies. How are you?"

Ambrosia answered for both. "We're fine, though I'm told the world beyond these walls is going mad."

Felicia held up a glass. "Fancy a drink? We're having sherry, but I could get you something stronger. Quite honestly, you look as if you could use it."

Basil ran a hand over his hair. "It was rather a stressful drive through the streets, but I'll collect on your offer in a while. I'm looking for Ginger. Have you seen her?"

"I believe she's in the bath," Felicia said. "She only just arrived herself, all hot and bothered, I'd say. I'm glad I chose to write from home today."

"Oh, well then," Basil said, stepping towards the drinks trolley. "I'll have that drink." He poured himself a brandy and chose an empty chair as far away from the two ladies as possible.

"How's your murder case?" Felicia asked, eyes wide with interest. She leaned towards Basil, "Perhaps you have something I could use in my next book?"

"Not all murders get solved," Basil said, "though it's not for lack of trying. Sometimes evidence simply eludes one."

"Don't tell me you're not going to solve the murder of Lord Whitmore?" Ambrosia said, the wrinkles on her face deepening with incredulousness.

Basil took a long sip of his brandy and relished the faint, sweet burn. "Never fear, Lady Gold, everything that can be done will be done."

He turned to Felicia. "I've brought Constable Braxton with me."

Felicia's glass stilled midway to her mouth. "What?

Why have you been withholding this information? Where is he?"

Basil's cheek twitched. "I picked him up off the street. He got caught up in a brawl and is a bit bloodied."

Felicia sprang to her feet. "Where is he? You didn't leave him in the stables or something ridiculous like that, did you?"

Basil couldn't help chuckling. "He's in good hands, dear girl, with Clement. I'm sure a visit from you would cheer him up."

Felicia discarded her near-empty glass and disappeared through the adjoining dining-room door that cut through to the kitchen.

Ambrosia wasn't pleased. "Must you encourage her?"

"I happen to think a match between a Gold lady and an officer of the law is a good one."

Ambrosia blew a breath through pursed lips, then muttered, "Time will tell."

Basil's life had certainly changed since he had married Ginger and moved into a house filled with strong-willed Gold women. Before they'd wed, he'd lived quietly and alone in a spacious townhouse in Mayfair.

Basil had had peace whenever he sought it, but it had come with the price of loneliness. Hartigan House buzzed with energy, and there was always something going on or someone to talk to, but it was also large enough that a man could find a corner to himself if he wanted it.

He finished his drink, rose to his feet, and smiled at the Dowager Lady Gold. "I'm going to see if Ginger has finished her bath. Would you like me to send someone to you?"

"I don't need monitoring. Besides, I can always ring the bell."

Basil left Ambrosia to herself and headed to the wide, curving staircase that led upstairs. Scout and the little dog were in full flight on the way down.

Basil jumped out of the way. "Whoa, what's the hurry?"

"Hello, Father," Scout said. He was red in the face, and his eyes sparkled, the image of health. It was hard to believe this was the same dirty, underfed lad who'd worked in steerage on the SS *Rosa* over the Atlantic.

"What are you off to in such a rush?"

"Oh, nowhere special. Boss and me are going to play with a ball in the back garden." Scout produced a small round ball as proof. Boss barked as if to endorse the lad.

"Very well, off you go, but no running in the house. You know the rules."

"Yes, Father."

Eager to have a word with Ginger, Basil took the rest of the steps two at a time. On opening the bedroom door, he stilled then smiled. Ginger, in only a negligée, hair damp, and her face free of makeup, was so beautiful, she took his breath away.

## 16

"*B*asil?"

Ginger had expected Lizzie to help her dress, not her husband, but he was much preferred.

Basil's lips pulled up crookedly as he stared at her, making her blush.

"Why are you looking at me like that?"

"Can't a man stare at his gorgeous wife?" He pulled her close and kissed her.

A knock on the door caused them to step apart. Lizzie's timing couldn't be worse.

"Madam?"

"Lizzie, thank you, but I'm not quite ready to dress. Mr. Reed and I are in the middle of a conversation."

"Yes, madam. I'll come back later." Lizzie bobbed, then added, "I have a message for Mr. Reed if you'll allow me."

"Of course," Ginger said. "What is it?"

"Constable Braxton is in the library with Miss Gold."

Ginger shot Basil a look of confusion.

"Yes, righto," Basil said. "Please tell him I'll join them shortly."

Lizzie dipped again and closed the door as she left.

Ginger tilted her head and raised a brow. "What is Constable Braxton doing here?"

Basil rubbed the back of his neck then settled into one of the gold and white striped chairs by the windows. "I found him in a tough situation in the street —this strike has got everyone on edge—and gave him a lift. I was, in fact, on the lookout for him."

Ginger lowered herself onto the stool in front of her dressing table. She might as well do her hair and makeup while they chatted.

"Oh?" she prompted.

"It's about this blasted case. I'm really at a loss as to what to do."

Ginger stared back at Basil's reflection. "And how does Constable Braxton fit in?"

"It's that Miss Darby. I can't help but think she's the key. The mistress often is."

Ginger's heart skipped as she held her hairbrush in mid-air. In a split second, she had to decide to keep the information she'd gained on her surveillance of Miss Gladys Darby to herself. Anything she learned from here on in, including confidences from Basil, had to be reported to Captain Smithwick. She swallowed the bile that formed in the back of her throat.

Ginger continued to brush her hair. "Miss Darby's rather aloof, and overconfident, if one might judge."

"It's that dratted alibi. But even if she didn't do the deed herself, she could lead me to who did."

"And what do you propose that Constable Braxton does?"

"I'm going to ask him to tail her. He's perfect for the job, you see. If she sees him, she'll simply try to seduce him." Basil laughed.

Ginger turned to face him with all seriousness. "I don't think Felicia will like that."

"No, I suppose not. Anyway, if Braxton is worth his grain of salt, he won't get caught out."

Ginger nibbled her bottom lip.

"What is it, love?"

"What?"

"You're working your lip. You always do that when something's troubling you."

"I do?" Ginger would need to watch herself in the future. It didn't do to have a "tell" as they said in poker.

Basil grinned. "You do."

"Well, it was nothing." Ginger ran her fingers through her bob to encourage it to dry. "I just think that maybe I'm a better candidate. For one, I have quite a bit of experience tailing people. I do a fair amount of that with my duties at Lady Gold Investigations. And two, there's no danger of my getting seduced, and therefore," she added a smile, "Felicia's feelings will be spared."

"You do make a good point. Except that you and she have already met, haven't you? You might catch her eye just as naturally for that reason."

Ginger turned back to the mirror and added mascara. It was important she didn't appear pushy, and yet, at the same time, vitally important that Constable Braxton didn't get pulled into the case. She'd hate for him to become a liability to the secret service. Lord knew what could happen then.

"With this strike," she began, "I would imagine Constable Braxton's talents could be used elsewhere, whereas I am rather up to date with all my duties."

Ginger twisted the mascara back into its tube, strolled over to her husband, and sat on his lap. "Let me do this for you, or else I might lose my sanity." She kissed his forehead.

"You drive a hard bargain, love."

She kissed his nose. "Is that a yes?"

"It's a yes," he said, then swooped her into his arms and headed for the bed, producing a fountain of giggles from her. "Now, where were we Mrs. Reed before your maid interrupted us?"

# 17

"*I*'ll be careful, I promise," Ginger reassured Basil as he kissed her goodbye the next morning.

"I'd start by watching her flat," Basil advised. "Make a note of when she comes and goes and the time."

"Yes, love."

"She's probably benign, but if she is indeed a femme fatale, she wouldn't think twice before harming you."

"Yes, love."

Basil touched his lips to her head. "And I couldn't bear it if anything happened to you."

"I'll be fine, I promise. I'll take every precaution. I'll even pull out one of my dark wigs and wear a frumpy frock."

"Fabulous idea!"

She watched through the French doors of the morning room as Basil headed down the path through the back garden to the garage, then went upstairs. Basil might have thought she'd come up with the disguise on the spur of the moment, but she'd already put her costume in a plain paper bag and concealed it in her wardrobe. Basil hadn't been gone ten minutes when Pippins tapped on her bedroom door.

"Yes?" Ginger said as she opened the door to the corridor.

"Madam, forgive my intrusion, but I thought you'd like to know that this came by messenger." Pippins handed her a white envelope with only Ginger's name and the word *PERSONAL* in capital letters on it.

"Thank you, Pippins."

Her butler bowed and walked away. Ginger closed the door before opening the sealed envelope with a long lacquered nail. Perhaps Captain Smithwick had someone watching her house? Otherwise, how did the messenger know that Basil had already gone?

There was no salutation on the white piece of paper, just two lines naming a hotel near the Cannon Street underground Station.

Another tap at the door startled her, and she quickly tossed the paper onto the coals burning in the fireplace.

"Come in," she said, standing so her body blocked the view of the fireplace from the doorway.

She'd expected that Pippins had returned, but this time her caller was Lizzie. She dipped with her head down and looked uncharacteristically nervous. Ginger gazed at her with curiosity, since she hadn't rung for the maid to come.

"What is it, Lizzie? Is everything all right below?"

"Yes, madam, it's just, I found this." Lizzie thrust out a hand that she'd kept behind her back and which held a printed flyer. She explained hurriedly as Ginger took it.

"I wasn't snooping, I swear. It was on the floor in the attic outside the bedroom of the newcomers."

Ginger lifted a brow. "The Bronsons?"

"Yes, madam. I wouldn't think anything about it, except, I didn't think you'd want a commie under your roof, madam."

The flyer contained communist propaganda used to entice people to join the party. Ginger had come across these memos in the past.

"Having one of these flyers doesn't automatically make one a communist."

Lizzie flushed a deep red. "No, madam, I just thought—"

"You did the right thing, bringing this to me, but

let's give Bronson and Mrs. Bronson the benefit of the doubt for now, shall we?"

"Yes, madam."

"And please keep this between us."

Lizzie dipped. "Yes, madam."

Ginger waited for Lizzie to leave then put the flyer into the top drawer of her dressing table. She dearly hoped Bronson had only been a carrier of the leaflet and not a distributor. Lizzie was right that Ginger didn't want to house a member of the Communist Party or be formally associated with the cause.

She slipped into a pair of black pumps and, before leaving the room, poked the remnants of the message from Captain Smithwick until they were entirely burned up. It wouldn't do for Basil to stumble across a piece of it by accident.

Ginger made an excuse to Clement about taking a taxicab instead of the Crossley, "The motor's rattling a bit. Would you mind looking?"

The weather had warmed up enough she could avoid wearing a jacket, which was why she had chosen a frock with long sleeves. Her cloche could be made plain-looking by simply removing the ribbon.

When the taxicab arrived, Ginger positioned herself in the back seat out of the direct line of sight of the rearview mirror. She opened the brown bag and, as an extra precaution, slipped low onto the seat, removed her cloche, and slipped on the wig. She'd already pinned her hair up at Hartigan House—her work having been concealed under the hat. She returned the brown cloche and then wiped off her rouge and lipstick with her handkerchief.

The cab driver deposited her at St. James's Park, not even giving her new appearance a second look, and she took the tube the rest of the way to Cannon Street. Now, as she stepped in with the other pedestrians, she relaxed her shoulders and let her chin sink into her chest, effectively disguising her gait. It'd been eight years since she was in active service, but it was like riding a bicycle. Balance came automatically once one pedalled.

## 18

*T*he hotel was an old, nondescript hovel, and Ginger immediately understood why Captain Smithwick had selected it. She ignored the lingering odour of stale cigarette smoke and dust. Without smiling, and with flawless French, she presented herself to the clerk, a middle-aged man with an overly long neck who barely suppressed a yawn.

*"Je suis Madame Margot Benac."*

The man's nose twitched. "Excuse me, madam, but it's English only in this 'ere fine establishment."

Ginger responded with a thick accent. "I am Madame Margot Benac. I arrive in this terribly congested and depressing city, and I want my room."

The clerk pushed a sign-in register towards her along with a pen and ink bottle. "It appears that a deposit has been put down on your be'alf for the week by a . . . er . . . Mr. Smith, who also 'as a key." He reappraised her as if he now shared an illicit secret, his eyebrows jumping.

Ginger signed the register with a flourish. Let the man think what he wanted.

"Room twelve," he said, "This is the only other key I 'ave. Yer lose it, yer 'ave to pay."

Ginger snatched the key from his hand.

He called after her. "Up the stairs and to your right."

It was fine that the clerk assumed that Ginger, as Margot Benac, was having romantic assignations with "Mr. Smith".

She snorted. Captain Smithwick should be so lucky.

The room was small with wooden floors and simple furnishings. A double bed with a wrought-iron frame, made up with thin sheets and pillows, sagged noticeably in the middle. Between the bed and window, a dusty round rug covered a small area. Ginger grunted under the effort it took to shimmy the window open, grateful for the sliver she managed and the bit of breeze that wafted into the stuffy room.

In the wardrobe hung an assortment of bland, dark-coloured frocks, unlike the clothing she or any fashionable French lady would ever wear socially, but perfectly suited to the leader of a Russian-led renegade club.

On the dressing table was a manila envelope, and inside were identification papers for Margot Benac that looked authentic. Beside it lay a small container resembling a jewellery box. Ginger opened it and smirked. Inside lay a rubber nose, a tube of mask glue, and face powder.

With nimble fingers, Ginger applied the prosthetic. She remembered back to the first time she had gone to such extremes to change her appearance, and how sticky her fingers had got and the mess she'd made of it. Now, she had the piece in place within minutes and used the powder to smooth out her complexion. A glance between her reflection in the mirror and the photograph in the identification papers reassured Ginger that her disguise was credible.

From the wardrobe, Ginger selected and changed into an oversized tweed spring jacket and then added a wide-brimmed hat, perfect for concealing the eyes. She replaced her two-inch pumps with flat tie-up shoes— just her size. How odd it felt to prepare to step out in public without heels. The only time she wore flat footwear was when she donned her slippers to travel from her bedroom to the loo at night.

Ginger had to duck to get her full length in the mirror and, satisfied that her transformation was complete, grabbed the old clutch bag Captain Smith-wick had provided, which contained her new identification and a few pounds she'd transferred over. Then, without hesitation, she left in search of Miss Darby and the mysterious leader of the presumed underground cell on Wallace Road.

GINGER WAS both amused and relieved. When she entered the same tea shop as the day before when she'd first kept eye on the entrance to the communist cell, the waitress behind the counter showed no signs of recognising her. No double-takes, no prolonged questioning looks. The same straightforward demeanour that, today for some reason, bordered on rude. She chose to order something different, requesting a croissant with butter and a dark coffee, "As dark as you can make it, made-moiselle," and returned to a window seat, not the same one, to watch the people outside.

It was already late morning, and Ginger, now knowing the routine with the hotel room and her costume, would be sure to arrive outside Miss Darby's building the next morning and follow her from there. For now, she could only hope that Miss Darby would return, or better, leave so Ginger could follow her to her next destination.

Ginger had developed an appetite and found she'd

nibbled through the delicious, flaky, and buttery croissant too quickly. She raised an arm and signalled a waitress to bring her another. Look at her, eating like a French woman!

Someone had left a copy of the day's *British Gazette* behind, and Ginger perused it, all the while keeping an eye on the door across the way.

## TWO HUNDRED BUSES ON CITY STREETS

The article claimed that transport in the city had begun to improve in light of all the buses. Ginger stared out at the congested street and could see only one wooden, red-painted bus, both its decks overloaded with passengers.

A pretty waitress delivered the second croissant, and without catching the girl's eye, Ginger slid a coin across the table in payment. She'd only taken one bite when the door in question opened. It wasn't Miss Darby, but a man exiting the door with his face concealed under a flat cap with the peak pulled low. Whoever it was could be part of the communist cell, and Ginger was determined to follow him.

Oh mercy, how she hated to leave the fresh croissant behind. Thinking quickly, she wrapped the pastry inside her handkerchief, clean except for the smudge of makeup, and hid it inside her handbag.

Keeping true to her slouchy gait, Ginger followed the man who'd exited the house.

The man walked quickly, almost sprinting, as he elbowed his way through the throng of annoyed pedestrians. Ginger kept several paces back but had to hurry to keep up. The bodies in front of her blocked her view of the man, and then a window between them would open giving her a glimpse only to then close again. Her heart beat with frustration.

A bump against her arm was followed by, "Watch it, lady!"

Ginger moved to the side, stepped up on her tiptoes, scoured the crowd ahead, but couldn't spot the flat cap. With a hand on her hip, she sighed heavily. How had she lost her mark so quickly? She was out of practice.

Then fortunes turned.

The man in the flat cap reappeared, and on his arm was Miss Darby herself!

Discreetly, Ginger followed the couple, though it wasn't hard with the crowds working as a shield. Miss Darby and the man in the cap turned down a narrow cobblestoned footpath between buildings, an area with fewer pedestrians, and Ginger had to keep a careful distance.

This lane, lengthy with sharp angles, had the couple disappear only to reappear as Ginger reached the corners. She nearly exposed herself when Miss Darby and the man made a sudden stop in front of a butcher's shop, the window dusty with a drawing of a side of beef etched on it and a dirty awning overhead that read Mason's Meats. Ginger pulled back just as the man's head lifted.

Ginger risked a peek in time to see the man lift a fist and knock on an obscure door. A distinct tapping rhythm, tap, tap, pause, tap, tap, pause, tap. After a short moment, the door opened, and the couple slipped inside.

Ginger released the breath she'd been holding. She waited, pretending to check a notebook, as other people scurried by. When no one else came knocking, Ginger hunched her shoulders, whispered to herself in French, *Je suis Madame Margot Benac,* approached the hard-to-see door, and using the same code, knocked.

A NARROW CORRIDOR ran past the shop at the front of the building to a door designed to look like a pantry shelf fitted with bowls and sundry items. Slightly open, the door led to a small room with an open-beam ceiling and a dozen wooden chairs, nearly all occupied. Ginger clasped her gloved hands together and stared back at the frowning faces.

"As I've already told your door boy," Ginger began

with a thick French accent, "I'm Madame Margot Benac. You are expecting me, no?"

An unshaven man wearing dark, unwashed clothes approached her with an extended hand, his expression guarded.

"Welcome to London. I'm Morton Ironside."

Ginger doubted that Ironside was the man's name, and her keen ear detected a slight Eastern European accent.

"My journey to zees city was *très* disagreeable and zee crowds uncontrollable," Ginger said sternly in a thickly French accent. "I hope my time here vill not prove to be wasted."

Mr. Ironside motioned to an empty chair near the front along the wall. With her practiced gait, Ginger crossed the room—avoiding eye contact with Miss Darby—and claimed the chair. It was in a good position, affording her a clear view of the room and its occupants.

The man who'd arrived with Miss Darby sat beside Mr. Ironside. He stood and began, "This unrest with the miners and the trade unions is a perfect storm of mass discontentment. Miner interest in our cause has never been greater. Our goal is to continue to stir up disillusion with the flawed ways of capitalism and the privileges for the aristocratic few. The bomb was a nice touch, eh?"

The crowd applauded, and Ginger joined in. If she learned nothing else, she now knew who'd been responsible for the bombing.

"Thank you, Mr. Milestone," Mr. Ironside said.

And now she had the name of the man in the flat cap.

When the murmurs died down, Mr. Ironside returned to Ginger. "Madame Benac, since you've come all this way, is there something you'd like to add?"

Ginger stood, her shoulders fell forward, and she ducked her chin so as to make the most use of the wide brim of her hat and the shadow it produced across her eyes.

"Merci, Mr. Ironside. Even with zee advancement of technology, it's difficult to provide secure communication between zee cells. How can we be sure zee telegrams, even coded, haven't been compromised? Zis we learned from zee Great War. Even as Mr. Ironside and Mr. Milestone are aliases, so ees Madame Benac. Our true identities are hidden to do zee work of secret intelligence. From what I see here, I can return to my hotel and relay a positive report."

Some stern expressions softened into slight smiles. From Ginger's peripheral vision, she saw Miss Darby who grinned with a glint in her eye. Had she seen through Ginger's ruse? Without an ounce of grace, Ginger lowered herself to her seat.

"Miss Darby?" Mr. Ironside began, "You have something to report?"

"Only that the mission was successful."

Mr. Ironside ducked his chin. "Very good."

*What mission? The assassination of Lord Whitmore?* Despite presumably being part of this network of cells, the real Madame Benac wasn't trusted enough by this group to be privy to details. Ginger would have to be patient if she meant to discover anything new enough to appease Captain Smithwick.

The meeting dispersed without fanfare, departures happening singly and in couples, not all at once but at timed intervals. Mr. Ironside had been the first to go, and Ginger wished she'd been able to get a name at least. The other man, Mr. Milestone, hovered beside her. He rocked on his heels.

He thrust out a rough hand. "My friends call me Fred."

Ginger took the man's hand tentatively.

"Never been to France," he said casually. "I've heard Nicolet is lovely."

Since there was no place by that name in all the country, it was obviously a test, "You're thinking of Nicolet, Quebec, in Canada, Mr. Milestone," Ginger said. "You must mean Nicole, in Aquitaine?"

"Indeed. Nicole. A slip of the tongue."

"Vill Mr. Ironside return?" she asked. "I vas hoping for a vord."

"If you've got something important to say, I can relay it for you. I'm Mr. Ironside's right-hand man."

"It's rather sensitive, meant for zee ears of zee cell leader only."

When Mr. Milestone failed to correct her or contradict her assumption, Ginger felt confident that Mr. Ironside was her man, Maxim Popov. No one else in the group had taken any type of leadership role, and everyone automatically deferred to Mr. Ironside.

She waited, hoping her silence would produce a titbit from her talkative friend, but as far as information on Mr. Ironside, Mr. Milestone was as tight as a drum. The fellow guarding the door caught her eye and tilted his head.

"*Après vous*, Madame?"

"Merci." Ginger left Mr. Milestone in her wake and stepped into the fresh air. Frustrated that she had learned nothing new, despite the massive effort to do so, she lumbered back to her hotel. Her fake nose was itchy, and she couldn't wait to take it off.

One couldn't, for one second, forget when one was operating as an alias, and Ginger was grateful for her training because when she turned the corner, she smacked into the back of a man.

"*Excusez-moi!*" she said.

The man stepped aside, and Ginger kept her gaze averted, not because Miss Darby stood in their midst, but because the man she was talking to was the journalist Mr. Tipper. Was he hot on the trail of a story, the same one she was on? Or was he somehow involved with the cell, and the spreading of communist propaganda? Though Mr. Tipper officially worked for the London News Agency, there were underground newspapers devoted to the Communist Party of Great Britain. Mr. Tipper might be a contributor using an alias or writing simply as anonymous.

Miss Darby pretended not to know Ginger as Madame Benac nor, one did hope, as Ginger Reed, and simply addressed the young man she herself was with on the pavement. Mr. Tipper's gaze showed no flicker of recognition, and he stepped into stride alongside Miss Darby.

By the time Ginger reached her room at the hotel, she had to take a moment to recline on the bed. She told herself it was to review what she'd learned, but the truth was, she simply hadn't slept well the night before and was utterly knackered.

To her disbelief, she nodded off and experienced a discombobulating moment when her eyelids flickered open, and she didn't immediately recognise her surroundings. When memory clicked in, so did her adrenaline. A quick look at her watch told her that she'd been out for almost an hour!

Forgetting about her nosepiece, she scratched at the itch it created, and the rubber prosthesis came off in her hand, making her jump.

*Oh mercy!*

Ginger raced to remove her costume and return to a version of herself. If she didn't connect with someone from home or work soon, questions about her whereabouts were sure to arise. Ignoring the front desk clerk, Ginger pushed the door and stepped onto the pavement. She was about to raise a hand to wave a taxicab down when she caught sight of a man leaning against the stone wall, bowler hat tilted on his head, and newspaper in his hand. He lowered the paper and grinned.

"Captain?" Ginger said stiffly.

Captain Smithwick folded the paper and tucked it under his arm. "Walk with me."

Ginger sighed in resignation then fell into step. "I'm afraid I don't have a lot to report." She relayed everything that had happened at the meeting of the communist cell.

"*Au contraire,*" he said with a perfect French accent. "You've learned the address of their meeting place and the English name of the cell leader. Morton Ironside."

"That's what he called himself."

Captain Smithwick repeated it, "*Morton Ironside. Rolls off one's tongue, does it not?*"

"I suppose."

Captain Smithwick waved down a taxicab that inched by, and Ginger thought it fortuitous that there was an empty one to wave down. The traffic travelled as if in slow motion. He opened the back door and instructed the cab driver, "Please take this lady to wherever she desires."

Ginger slid into the backseat, then Captain Smithwick closed the door, banging the black top of the vehicle in signal to the driver she was ready to go.

Even with rubber tyres, the taxicab jerked along the cobbled and uneven road. Overfilled buses moved like slugs in the rain with passengers leaning over the rails of the open-air second decks. One zoomed precariously around a corner, and Ginger worried the vehicle would tip over. Mercifully, it continued upright and the passengers were spared a dreadful shock.

The streets were often deadlocked with angry pedestrians, shoulder-to-shoulder, pulsating down overfilled pavements and blocking traffic to cross at inopportune junctions. Ginger wondered if it might not be faster for her to walk back to Kensington!

The air was thick with discontent, and it wouldn't take long for a mob to form and start trouble. If the recent bombing was the only destructive event to come from the general strike, then perhaps the citizens of London should consider themselves lucky.

The lengthy journey home gave Ginger time to reflect on all that had happened, especially the latest encounter with Leo Tipper and Gladys Darby. What was the journalist's involvement with Miss Darby? They hadn't acted like lovers, even ones engaged in a spat. Were they co-conspirators? Had Mr. Tipper led Ginger to believe the relationship was romantic to throw her off the scent?

As they drove, Ginger removed her wig and the hairpins, fluffing out her red bob. When Hartigan House finally came into view, Ginger retrieved the fare from her handbag and topped it off with a generous tip.

For the first time since Ginger got into his vehicle, the taxicab driver smiled. "Thank you, madam. Hopefully, this strike will end soon, and we can get ourselves back to normal, eh?"

Once inside, Ginger flagged down Lizzie. "Is Master Scout upstairs?"

"I believe he's outside with Mr. Fulton and Miss Gold."

Ginger raised a brow at that combination. Once Scout's lessons were completed, Mr. Fulton usually left for the university to fulfil his duties there.

Not yet ready to take the time to change out of her plain frock, Ginger instead covered it with an attractive spring coat she'd left behind in her study. In the garden, she found Clement's nephew actively trimming hedges. "Hello, Mr. Bronson," she said as she approached. "How are you getting on here at Hartigan House?"

"Good afternoon, madam." He wiped his forehead with the back of his hand. "Things are going well. I must thank you again for taking me and the missus on and at such short notice."

"It's a serendipitous affair for us both. You needed work, and I needed workers. I'm pleased to be able to help Clement's family members. We are very fond of him here."

"He speaks very highly of you, madam, and all of the family. Especially the lad, Master Scout."

Ginger couldn't stop the smile that took over her face. "I'm rather fond of the lad as well. Have you seen him about?"

"I believe he's in the stable, madam."

"Of course. It's what I would expect.

Mr. Bronson smiled faintly and bowed his head.

Scout was indeed found in the stables along with Felicia and Mr. Fulton, and of course, Boss, who, when Ginger wasn't around, stayed loyally at Scout's side.

"Hello there," Ginger said as she stepped inside.

"Ginger?" Felicia returned. "Did you know that Mr. Fulton rides?"

Scout jumped in. "He's got a horse!"

Ginger smiled. "I didn't know."

"He's promised to let me ride it one day."

"If you will permit it," Mr. Fulton said. "She's more my sister's horse than mine, but my parents keep the mare in their stables, so I'm free to ride her at any time."

"Scout was eager to show off Goldmine and Sir Blackwell," Felicia said. "I thought I'd tag along."

Ginger smirked. Felicia's love for horses ended at Ascot once she'd shown off her latest fascinator, the famous hat style ladies wore to Ascot races that were more like art deco for one's head than anything meant to protect a lady from the sun. Charming Mr. Fulton was the enticement for Felicia's recent interest, Ginger was certain.

Ginger patted Goldmine's shimmering blond flank. "And what do you think, Mr. Fulton?"

"Stunning, Mrs. Reed." Mr. Fulton's dark eyes glistened with admiration. "I'd heard of the breed but never had the privilege of seeing one up close."

Ginger nuzzled her gelding's neck. "Goldmine is a treasure in every way."

"Can I take Mr. Fulton riding, Mum?" Scout stared with earnest expectation. "He can ride Sir Blackwell."

Mr. Fulton blushed. "I wouldn't think of imposing."

"It's not an imposition," Ginger said. "The horses need their exercise. It would be a help to me if you could. I'm afraid I've been rather busy of late and dreadfully neglectful."

Mr. Fulton's shoulders relaxed. "If you don't mind, madam, it would be my pleasure."

"Not a long one, mind?" Ginger said. "Please return before dark."

"Of course." Mr. Fulton turned to Scout, "What tack belongs to Sir Blackwell?"

Boss had been nosing about the hay, and Ginger called for him, so he wouldn't inadvertently get stepped on. With her pet safely cradled in her arms, she returned to the house.

Felicia stepped in after her. "Terrific. What am I to do now?"

Ginger laughed. "Do I detect a note of jealousy?"

"I do declare, of what?"

"That Mr. Fulton has chosen to spend his afternoon with Scout rather than you?"

"Well, he did just spend the whole morning with the lad."

"What about Constable Braxton?"

"What about him?"

Ginger stopped and looked Felicia in the eye. "I do

believe you've given him the impression that the two of you are stepping out."

"I have not."

Ginger raised a brow. "Are you certain?"

"Can't a girl just have a bit of fun?"

"You sound very American right now."

Felicia folded her arms. "What's wrong with that? American girls are footloose and fancy-free. English girls are old even when they're young."

Ginger called into the kitchen to order a tray of sandwiches before heading to the sitting room. She was jolly well ready for a drink and very happy to find that Basil had come home in the meantime and was waiting there.

Ginger greeted him with a kiss. "I didn't see you drive in."

"Braxton dropped me off. Brandy?"

"Please." Placing Boss on the carpet, Ginger sat on the settee and slipped off her shoes. At the sideboard, Basil poured two drinks, handed one to Ginger, and settled in beside her.

"How's the case going?" Ginger asked before Basil could ask her about her day, a question that would force her to be as vague as possible.

Basil let out a long sigh. "I'm hitting a dead end at

every turn, I'm afraid. No one seems to know anything of value, or at least if they do, they're not talking. The House of Lords doesn't take a suspicious death of one of their own lying down, and Morris is breathing down my neck to solve it quickly."

Ginger noted the rings of worry under Basil's eyes and the deepening of the lines on his face. In the past, Ginger would have shared the new information she'd gained and would have worked tirelessly alongside Basil to help him solve his cases.

How hypocritical of her to have lectured Felicia about loyalty and trust when she was deceiving her own husband!

Lizzie arrived with the plate of sandwiches Ginger had requested.

"Thank you, Lizzie," she said.

Her maid bobbed. "You're welcome, madam. Is there anything else?"

"That will be all," Ginger said. She could always ring the bell if she thought of something they needed later.

The pang she felt at her own shortcomings as a wife hadn't affected her appetite, and Ginger helped herself to several triangles of cheese and cucumber sandwiches.

A tap on the door was followed by Pippins' balding

head. "I'm sorry to interrupt, but there's a telephone call for you, Mr. Reed. It's Scotland Yard."

Ginger was too comfortable with her feet up and half a glass of brandy in her stomach to follow him this time. Whatever the urgency was, Basil, always faithful and loyal, would report it to her. She let her head fall back and allowed her eyelids to close.

She startled back to life when she heard Basil lumber back into the room. He stared at her with a grim look on his face.

"What is it, love?" Ginger asked.

"There's another body."

## 19

*G*inger pursed her lips in interest.

Basil knew her well and gave her a little teaser. "The body was found in a service lane. Middle-aged male."

Under normal circumstances, she'd jump at the chance to visit the scene of the crime, especially during slow periods at Lady Gold Investigations. Even then, much of what was requested from her involved surveillance, which Felicia had become adept at doing. Basil raised a brow in anticipation of her next comment, a request to tag along, but she held her tongue. Her focus must be entirely on the communist cell and gaining information about their next moves, and if they had any nefarious intentions.

She deflected by saying, "Aren't you busy with Lord Whitmore's investigation?"

Basil lifted a shoulder. "Henderson is laid up with a stomach ailment, so Morris wants me to attend. There was a driving licence on the corpse which hopefully will make things easier."

He glanced at the note in his hand. "A Frederick Milestone."

Ginger had been on the cusp of making an excuse about feeling a tad under the weather herself but stopped at the mention of the dead man's name. Frederick Milestone? Could it be the same man she'd only just spoken to that morning at the communist cell?

"Sounds interesting," she said casually while slipping her shoes back on. "I'm rather idle. Mind if I join you?" She didn't have to mew about staying out of the way of the police and all that. She'd proven her mettle for observation and investigation enough times in the past to quiet even the brash Superintendent Morris.

Basil's wrist flicked as he checked his watch. "We'd better get a move on before it gets too dark to see anything."

"I'm right behind you. Just let me get my hat and gloves."

Ginger hurried to her study, collected her hat and gloves, but took a quick moment to jot down a note, seal it in an envelope and scribble out the address Captain Smithwick had given her. She tucked it in her handbag, then purposely left the handbag behind.

In the back garden, Basil took long strides to the garage.

"Oh, love," Ginger said. "I've forgotten my handbag. I'll only be a second."

Basil's look of annoyance was fleeting. "I'll back out the Austin."

Inside, Ginger collected her handbag and rang for Pippins. "Please arrange for this to be delivered as soon as possible," she instructed.

Pippins, with his left hand tucked behind his back, received the envelope with his right and bowed. "Right away, madam."

Ginger sprinted out of the back entrance to the garden to make up for lost time.

She jumped into the passenger seat and smiled apologetically at her husband. "So sorry, love."

She *was* sorry. The lie sat uncomfortably in her belly like a thick glob of glue.

Basil was an efficient driver, manoeuvring around traffic jams and taking short cuts through lesser-known lanes. Ginger's pulse sped up as they reached their destination, as it wasn't so far from the area she'd been watching earlier that day. Basil pulled up to where several black police vehicles were parked.

GINGER'S HEART was a twisted knot. If Captain

Smithwick hadn't interfered with her life, she'd be sharing everything she knew, every intuition she had, every concern. Feeling wretched, she remained inexplicably quiet. If Basil noticed, he kept his thoughts to himself. Ginger was grateful he had been preoccupied with the snarled-up traffic, and he even swore once having hit a pile of horse dung head-on. Dusk approached, and Basil turned on the headlights.

The service alley was a mess of brambles poking through old fencing and overflowing rubbish bins. Ginger placed a gloved finger under her nose as she exited the motorcar to avoid sniffing the stench. Basil left the headlights on to light up the scene.

Dr. Wood was already there and greeted Ginger and Basil with a sombre look.

"Hello, Chief Inspector, Mrs. Reed," he said. On the side of the road, the corpse was on his stomach, the cause of death apparent. A butcher's cleaver had been inserted cleanly into his back. Though the man's face was partially concealed, Ginger could confirm this was the body of the man she'd known as Frederick Milestone.

Constable Braxton, already on the scene, jogged over to join them.

"Sir, Mrs. Reed," the constable said, then back to Basil. "The men are scouring the area, but there's nothing out of the ordinary so far."

Basil nodded then faced the pathologist. "I take it, he died as a result of the knife in his back."

Dr. Wood concurred. "The knife intersected the heart. Death would've been instantaneous."

Basil hummed. "The question is . . . was the attack random or was this man targeted?"

Most definitely targeted, Ginger thought, but once again, she kept her thoughts to herself.

Basil coughed into his fist. "Dreadful stench."

"I believe that's coming from the butcher's shop waste," Constable Braxton said.

"How long has the man been dead?"

"Rigor hasn't even started," Dr. Wood stated. "Less than four hours."

Ginger concurred with the time since she'd seen the man in person not long before that.

As Basil squatted to examine the man, Ginger scoured the immediate area, careful not to get in the way of the other officers on site. Amongst the litter, she spotted a folded, faded red flyer with the familiar communist markings—the same propaganda Clement's nephew Harold Bronson had allegedly had in his possession. She glanced about. Basil's back was to her, and the constables were conferring. She scooped up the flyer and slipped it into her handbag. She didn't want Basil to make a connection between this death and the communist cell.

"Perhaps he's part of a gang," she offered when she returned to Basil's side. It was an intentionally misleading comment, and Ginger's stomach clenched.

Basil, on his feet again, scribbled onto his notepad.

"The initials M.M. are scratched into the handle of the cleaver."

Ginger swallowed dryly. M.M. *Masons Meats*. Basil was a clever detective and eventually this evidence would lead him to the communist cell front, and there was nothing Ginger could do about it. She had to get there first.

Her thoughts returned to Mr. Milestone's body. Why would anyone want to kill him? Had he betrayed Morton Ironside in some way? Were other members' lives in danger? Gladys Darby?

"Tell me, darling," Ginger started, "did you ever speak to Miss Darby again?"

Basil shot her a look.

"Something reminded me of Lord Whitmore. Now that you have this new case, I hope Lord Whitmore won't be forgotten."

Basil looked stricken, and Ginger felt like a heel. "I'm sorry, love, I didn't mean that you would forget. I know a lot is going on at the Yard with the strike and everything, that's all."

"Yes, well, I'm doing what I can along with all the officers in the city. And to answer your question, no, I haven't spoken to Miss Darby since the time she was in my office."

"I'm sure you're needed there." Ginger waved an arm. "I can take a taxicab home."

Basil narrowed his eyes in question. "Are you sure?"

"I'm feeling rather tired, and I've work waiting for me in my study."

"Taxicabs are running slowly."

"Not much slower than you can go, love. I promise. I'll be fine."

"All right. If you're certain." Basil kissed her quickly on the forehead. "I'll see you back at Hartigan House."

Ginger waited until Basil disappeared through the crowd on his way back to his motorcar, and she waved down a taxicab.

"Where to, miss?"

Ginger debated for a split second then gave the address for Miss Darby's flat on Fleet Street.

## 20

The streets had cleared as the business day had ended. Pedestrians—either frustrated businessmen, shoppers, or disgruntled rabble-rousers—had been compelled to obey their stomachs and search for their tea.

A rustle of branches caused Ginger to still. The darkness worked to conceal other people as well, and Ginger had a fleeting thought that someone might be following her. Staying close to a parked lorry, she waited. After she had released a breath, tilted her head down, and glanced over her shoulder, she headed into Miss Darby's building.

The radio played loudly behind Mr. Savage's door, which convinced Ginger that the man was hard of hearing and that anyone could have slipped by and gone to Miss Darby's flat without his knowing.

LEE STRAUSS

On the next floor, Ginger knocked on Miss Darby's door. She waited but couldn't hear footsteps or any signs of life. No light sneaked out from the crack under the door.

"Miss Darby?"

Evidence of Lord Whitmore's death would've been cleared away, and Ginger feared she might find another body behind the door. Whoever had killed Mr. Milestone might be after Miss Darby.

Ginger knocked more firmly. "Miss Darby?"

When Miss Darby failed to answer, Ginger's fingers went to the pins in her hat. Even though a cloche hat never needed pinning, Ginger felt it expedient to include a couple in the decor. You never knew when you might need to pick a lock.

The corridor was empty, and Ginger worked the lock with two hatpins until she heard the bearings click. At the same moment, a door down the hall opened, and Ginger slipped into the darkness of Miss Darby's flat in the nick of time. She held her breath until the heavy footsteps of a man faded away down the stairs.

Ginger retrieved a small torch from her handbag and flashed it about. If someone watched from outside, Ginger didn't want to give herself away by flicking on the electric lights.

"Miss Darby?" she whispered, but there was no response.

Through the narrow beam of her torchlight, Ginger confirmed that the living and kitchen areas were unoccupied, along with the bedroom.

The door to the bathroom was partially closed. The gruesome scene of Lord Whitmore's pink body in the bathtub flashed through her mind. Her imagination produced a copy, only this time with Miss Darby lying in the bath.

Ginger's pulse raced as she pushed open the bathroom door. A windowless room, she risked pulling the cord to switch the light on. The bulb brightened the small space, forcing her to momentarily close her eyes against it. She let out a breath of relief. Miss Darby was not to be found there.

*Where was she?*

Once outside, Ginger hailed another taxicab and didn't ask to be taken home. She needed to contact Captain Smithwick. The nearest private telephone was at her Lady Gold Investigations office.

GINGER PAID the taxicab driver and walked quickly to the door of her office. She paused when she saw the lights on inside. Felicia rarely stayed this late, but

LEE STRAUSS

sometimes, she was excited about her writing and would lose track of time.

Checking the handle, Ginger found the door was unlocked. She'd have to talk to Felicia about locking herself inside if she was going to stay after dark.

"Felicia, love?"

Felicia sat behind her desk, a sheet of paper in the roller of her typewriter. "Since I was unable to join Scout and Mr. Fulton on their outing, I decided to make use of my free time to work on my book. And good thing," she added, pointing to the man sitting in one of the chairs in front of Ginger's desk. "We've got a client."

Ginger's blood ran cold. Staring back with a crooked grin was Mr. Ironside, also known, she was certain, as Maxim Popov.

Ginger arranged her features as if she were only mildly surprised to see a guest and not experiencing the awful dread she was feeling. Did Maxim Popov know her as Ginger Reed? Had they ever met?

No, she was reasonably certain they hadn't, though he might know who she was from the society papers.

"Oh, hello." She extended a gloved hand. "I'm Mrs. Reed, also known as Lady Gold."

Maxim Popov returned her handshake politely.

"This is Mr. Ironside," Felicia said. She stared at Ginger with a blank expression. "He insisted on waiting. I left a message with Pippins." Felicia broke into a smile. "Your speed in getting here has to be a record, even for you."

"Yes, well, as serendipity would have it, I was actually in the area and came of my own accord without receiving your message."

Ginger removed her gloves and hat and sat on her desk chair opposite Mr. Popov.

"How might I be of service to you, Mr. Ironside?"

Mr. Popov didn't flinch. "I've heard that you're quite accomplished at uncovering secrets, Mrs. Reed."

Ginger laughed girlishly. "I don't know about that. I suppose a little snooping around comes with the territory." She held his gaze boldly. "Why, is there something you'd like to uncover?"

Mr. Popov leaned back, crossed his legs, and retrieved a cigarette case from his suit pocket. "Do you mind if I smoke?"

Ginger ducked her chin. She did mind, but she perceived that more significant battles were coming her way. "Not at all."

Felicia stared at Ginger, wide-eyed, from her position behind Mr. Popov's back. "Should I make tea?"

Ginger smiled reassuringly. "That would be splendid." Whatever Mr. Popov was about to say, Ginger would rather Felicia wasn't privy to it.

The man struck a match, puffed on the cigarette as

he lit it, and the tip glowed red. Flicking his wrist, he extinguished the flame and slowly blew smoke in her direction. A compelling performance, Ginger thought.

"Mr. Ironside?" she prompted.

"Yes, I'm actually looking for a woman. A French woman." He eyed her carefully. "She goes by the name Madame Margot Benac."

Ginger was instantly transported back to a moment in France when she'd been confronted by a German officer who'd begun to doubt her identity. The interview then had been interrupted before he could follow through on his veiled threat. Captain Smithwick had reassigned her the next day.

"I don't believe I know who she is," Ginger said calmly.

The crooked grin reappeared. "Are you sure? I believe she's been sighted at Mason's Meats. You've been there, surely."

"No. My cook makes all our meat purchases from a shop in Kensington."

Mr. Popov sniffed. "I see."

Felicia returned with the tea, and played mother, pouring for all three and offering milk and sugar.

"I hope I haven't missed anything important," she said. "I will take notes if necessary."

To Ginger's dismay, Mr. Popov turned his attention to Felicia. Maxim Popov had a certain masculine magnetism and quite charmed the ladies when he wanted to.

"Thank you, Miss Gold," he said. "Such a lovely secretary you have, Mrs. Reed." He shot a look at Ginger before smiling widely at Felicia. "I don't suppose one as lovely as you would be unattached?"

Felicia blushed, pushed a dark lock of hair behind her ear, and batted thick lashes. Ginger had seen her in operation with the opposite sex many times before and couldn't stop the wave of anxiety building in her chest.

"I'm not officially spoken for, Mr. Ironside. But," Felicia glanced at Ginger, who flashed her a sharp no-flirting-with-clients glare. "I'm rather busy writing books. And working here . . ." She let the thought dangle.

Maxim Popov extinguished his cigarette in the ashtray Felicia had provided and took a sip of his tea.

"Perfect, Miss Gold. The tea is perfect. You are a lady of many talents."

"Thank you, Mr. Ironside."

Ginger cleared her throat. "As to your missing French woman, I don't think I'm the right person to assist you. Perhaps I can make a recommendation."

Mr. Popov slowly lowered his teacup, set it on the matching saucer, and set it on the table.

"Actually, I think you're the very best person to help me, Mrs. Reed." His glance returned to Felicia, his eyes smiling, but when his gaze returned to Ginger, all mirth disappeared. "I would hate for anyone to get hurt."

Ginger didn't miss the veiled threat. He swivelled back to Felicia. "Pretty young ladies such as yourself need to be extra cautious at night. Perhaps I can accompany you home? Make sure you get there safely."

Ginger jumped in before Felicia could respond. "We're quite capable of getting home on our own."

"Yes, well," Mr. Popov got to his feet and held out his hand. Ginger hesitated before accepting it. Without her gloves, she felt the roughness of Maxim Popov's palm and the firmness of his grip. "I'd be delighted if you visited the shop in question, just to see what you can find out."

"Like I said—"

"Perhaps now, on your way home?"

It sounded like a question, but Ginger could see the warning in Maxim Popov's eyes. If she wanted Felicia to stay safe, she'd better do what he wanted.

And just in case she misinterpreted his meaning, the communist cell leader carefully opened the flap of his jacket to reveal the hammer end of a pistol jutting from the waistline of his trousers.

## 21

"Is everything all right, Ginger?" Felicia carefully stacked the loose sheets of her manuscript and placed them in her desk drawer. "You look unsettled."

Ginger plastered on a smile. The outline of Maxim Popov's pistol in his suit pocket registered clearly in her mind. Just out of Felicia's line of sight, the man waited for her in the reception area.

Unfortunately, Ginger's own pistol, a palm-sized Remington Derringer, a gift from her late husband, Daniel, was tucked away in the bottom locked drawer of her desk, and woefully out of reach.

"Everything's fine," Ginger replied. "I just think I should pop into Feathers & Flair while I'm here."

"I'm afraid I can't wait for you." Felicia slipped her arms into her jacket. "I've promised Constable Braxton

I'd have dinner with him tonight. And no, before you launch into another lecture, I'm not trifling with his feelings. He knows I'm undecided."

"So long as he knows." Ginger's gaze flickered to the door where Maxim Popov inclined his head sharply. When Ginger reached for her coat and handbag, he shook his head sharply, his pistol now in full view.

Ginger hurried to beat Felicia out. "You don't mind locking up, then?"

Felicia pouted. "I am rather in a hurry. I had to wait with Mr. Ironside."

"It'll only take you a minute. I promised Madame Roux."

Felicia huffed; her eyes riveted to the paper rolled into her typewriter. "Fine."

Maxim Popov, in a seemingly gentlemanly manner, held the door open for her then gripped her elbow and led her to a dark automobile. Ginger worked to keep her stride natural.

"You can drive," he said.

Ginger was about to protest when he added tersely. "I know you are quite capable, Mrs. Reed."

Ginger took her position behind the large steering wheel while Maxim Popov angled his body to face her, his pistol in clear view.

"I'm not familiar with this model," Ginger said. "How does one turn on the headlights?"

"There's a button on the left."

"To the butcher's shop," Maxim Popov instructed. "And no funny stuff or an innocent may die, and his blood will be on your head."

Ginger didn't doubt for a moment that the Russian would follow through on such a threat as that.

Ginger swallowed hard, her throat dry with nerves. After-hours traffic wasn't as heavy and soon she was motoring through Piccadilly Circus, weaving past horse-drawn carriages and trailing other motorcars closely. It wasn't likely that her driving would gain her any attention, other than the random blasting of horns from irritated drivers, a sound Ginger just equated with driving through London.

"Got a heavy foot, eh?" Popov said. "Remember what I said about silly business."

Ginger eased up on the pedal. There was no reason to get to where Popov wanted to take her in a hurry.

Popov kept his pistol trained on Ginger, his other hand nervously on the dashboard.

"You wonder how I know about you?" he said, a teasing glint in his dark eyes. Ginger, in fact, did wonder.

"Yes," Popov continued, "your impersonation of Madame Benac was quite good indeed, but not quite good enough. You see, I met her once, years ago, but even with age, I would know her again. We were . . . er . . . close once," he grinned slyly. "If you know what I mean."

Ginger groaned inwardly. Captain Smithwick's intelligence providers had missed this vital piece of information.

"Then you must also know that I've been out of service since the war. You have me mistaken for someone else."

Popov laughed heartily. "You take me for a fool, Mrs. Reed. Believe me, I'm no fool. Your Whitmore fellow thought me a fool as well."

Ginger feigned confusion at Trafalgar Square, Nelson's column towering overhead, and circled more than once.

"Lord Whitmore never confided in me. You'd do better talking to Miss Darby about that."

Maxim Popov clicked his tongue. "Talk about losing one's edge. The fact that your agency kept Whitmore in action is a sign of capitalistic incompetence." His crooked grin spread. "You will see communism sweep this pathetic island in your lifetime, Mrs. Reed."

"I doubt that," Ginger replied. Not only because she refused to believe communism would rule, but because she knew that, barring a miracle, Maxim Popov wouldn't let her live to see the day.

She felt a sense of crushing heartache that she hadn't experienced since Daniel had died—remorse at missing Scout growing into a young man, devastation at bringing pain to Basil, and sadness at the confusion he'd experience not understanding why she'd died.

In the midst of the bustling Covent Garden district just past the Savoy, a lorry cut in front of their motorcar and Ginger slammed on the brake, causing them both to jerk forward.

"Mrs. Reed! I've warned you!"

"The lorry cut in front of me."

"Your driving is extraordinarily erratic."

Ginger flashed him a look of offence. "This is how I drive!"

However, the errant lorry gave Ginger an opportunity, and she faked losing control of the steering, hitting the edge of the pavement head-on, and going straight into a lamp post.

Ginger wasted no time jumping out of the motorcar and prayed her Italian leather pumps would stand up to a good jog.

Popov called, "Mrs. Reed!"

Serendipitously, a dog took that moment to release

LEE STRAUSS

the load that nature had given him, and Ginger heard Popov swear as he stepped in it.

The distraction gave Ginger a chance to slip into a side street, though the sounds of a gun going off—or was it a vehicle backfiring?—made her flinch.

The alley was empty except for a few long shadows cast by the odd electric street lamp. Ginger could risk re-entering the main street. Since she hadn't taken her coat, she had nothing left to remove to help disguise herself, and she couldn't very well remove her frock! Hailing a taxicab would be too revealing, as would waiting about for a bus. Her best bet was to disappear into the underground and mingle with the crowds there, but the nearest station, Charing Cross, was several streets away.

Ginger slammed herself against a brick wall at the sound of voices, then let out a breath as a romantic couple holding hands strolled through, giggling together in a shallow world of love-induced oblivion.

"Mrs. Reed!"

Popov!

Ginger held still against the wall, but the light from a nearby gas lamp wasn't situated in her favour. A gun blast took off the edge of a brick above her head. Ginger ducked and began to sprint.

Her heart pounded loudly in her chest, but not

loudly enough to block out the terrifying sound of quick footsteps growing close.

Drat these Italian pumps! Ginger should've discarded them when she had a chance. She almost made it to the corner, almost able to throw herself on the mercy of whatever spectators and passers-by there would be, almost able to stop traffic, before Popov's strong hand gripped her arm and pulled her back into the shadows. A second tug and her arm was winched painfully behind her back, and the nose of his pistol was digging into her ribs. His breath was hard and heavy in her ears.

"I have one bullet left, Mrs. Reed. It's up to you if I use it now."

Ginger hardly felt that her death in the alley would be of any advantage to her, and even though she was certain her ultimate demise was Maxim Popov's intention, she couldn't give up without a fight. Time might give her another chance.

"No need," she said, forcing a light tone.

"Now that you've wrecked my motorcar, we'll have to walk to our destination. Are you up to the added exercise, Mrs. Reed?"

"Most certainly, Mr. Ironside."

By the time Ginger and Popov had reached the

butcher's shop, Ginger's feet ached. After an hour of walking, and one pump heel broken, a massive blister had formed. If her life hadn't been in imminent danger, she'd be sincerely mourning her ruined Italian shoes.

Popov, his pistol still on Ginger's back, pushed a key into her hand. "Open it."

Ginger wrestled with the key, finding the keyhole sticky, her mind working to find a solution. Once she was forced inside, her options would be limited indeed, but there wasn't much one could do with a pistol pressed against one's back.

Popov applied more pressure. "Hurry up!"

Left without a choice, Ginger relented, silently praying that Captain Smithwick had got the message she'd sent through Pippins. After a click, the door swung open. Popov called out, "Miss Darby, are you here?"

Ginger felt a flash of alarm. If Mr. Popov had killed Mr. Milestone, he wouldn't hesitate to kill Miss Darby.

Miss Darby materialised, reached toward the wall and flicked on a light. Ginger glanced at her with a look of apprehension and wished she could convey hope that the two of them, acting wisely, could outwit and overpower their captor. But Miss Darby wouldn't hold her gaze.

Was Gladys Darby under Popov's command? Did he have some kind of hold on her? Blackmail? A threat?

Ginger stumbled down the corridor, one shoe lower than the other, as Popov mercilessly pushed her along. The room behind the pantry door was dank in its plain decor and the lingering smell of raw meat that filtered in from the butchers. The chairs, vacant and askew, seemed to mock her.

"Miss Darby, the rope. Tie Mrs. Reed's hands behind her back. *Securely.*"

Maxim Popov trained his pistol on Ginger, and she grimaced as Miss Darby bound her wrists. Surely, she'd leave them loose, so she could free herself later, but it appeared she took Mr. Popov's command seriously.

It didn't take her long to learn why. As soon as she was bound, Miss Darby pushed Ginger, forcing her to sit in one of the wooden chairs. Then she smiled. "Hello, *Madame Benac.*"

Ginger's heart sank. Gladys Darby and Maxim Popov were on the same team.

Miss Darby threw salt into the wound by walking to Maxim Popov and planting a kiss on his lips.

She gazed up at him with a look of admiration. "Should we just kill her now?"

"Patience, *milaya.* She may be of use to our cause. What they call leverage."

"Ack," Miss Darby said with an air of disgust.

Ginger winced at the bite of the ropes on her

wrists. She glared at Maxim Popov. "What do you want with me now?"

"I want to know your secrets, of course."

"What kind of secrets? I don't know anything."

"Of course, you do, Madame Benac. Or do you prefer Mademoiselle LaFleur?"

Ginger caught her breath. Antoinette LaFleur was the alias she'd used during the war.

He chuckled. "The British isn't the only government with an intelligence agency."

Oh, mercy. How much did Maxim Popov know about her?

The amusement in Popov's expression vanished. "You've lost your edge, agent. I can practically read your mind. Your eyes give everything away."

Ginger clenched her jaw.

Popov lifted his chin in Miss Darby's direction. "Fetch me a glass of water." His eyes narrowed on Ginger. "It was a long walk here."

"What happened to the motorcar?" Miss Darby asked, her mouth agape.

"Mrs. Reed decided to drive it into a lamp post."

Miss Darby pierced Ginger with a look of rage. "Why, you minx!"

"Calm down," Popov said. "It can be fixed. Now get me my water."

Ginger's eyes drifted about the room. Besides the

empty chairs, there was a table topped with an empty vodka bottle and three toppled glasses, and a portable cabinet with one door askew, but not opened far enough for Ginger to see the contents. Built of stone, the only light emanating from the back room came from a single bulb hanging from a rafter. There were no windows.

No windows, and from Ginger's perspective at the moment, no way out.

Maxim Popov interrupted her thoughts. "Who is your commander?"

"I'm sorry?"

"Who sent you to me?" He flicked a hand at the room. "How did you find me?"

This was Ginger's chance to bluff.

"I don't know the name of my recruiter. An anonymous letter came to me in the post, commanding me to step back into service."

"Commanding you?"

Ginger tilted her head defiantly. "Yes, commanding."

"How very undiplomatic of your government."

"It's what I agreed to when I signed up back in '15. They already knew about you and this cell in London, and obviously, about Madame Benac. When I don't report back at the appointed time, they will send out a search party. They're probably on their way here now."

Maxim Popov laughed. "I see it now. You're a good agent. Any chance you'd like to work for us? We could use a double agent, and the money . . ." He rubbed two fingers together. "I could barter a good deal for you."

"I'm a wealthy lady already, Mr. Popov."

It was the first time Ginger had used Maxim Popov's real name, and she felt a strong sense of satisfaction when his eyes flickered with surprise.

"So, you know who I am?"

"We *all* know who you are."

Mr. Popov's eyes calculated the enormity of this statement, and Ginger took a chance.

"You're not only responsible for the recent bombing, but for the deaths of Lord Whitmore and your agent known as Milestone."

Mr. Popov showed signs of being rattled, and Ginger's lip twitched with gratification. She hadn't been sure if Mr. Popov had been complicit in the murders, but now she knew.

Miss Darby returned with a glass of water and Popov made a show of taking a long drink. Ginger's throat felt like sandpaper, and she couldn't help but watch with longing.

Wiping his mouth with the back of his sleeve, Popov rubbed it in. "That was good. But you know what I need now? A Coca-Cola. Another amazing American invention, is it not, Mrs. Reed? Don't you just love how the cold bubbles quench the thirst? There's nothing like it." He waved dismissively at Miss Darby. "Gladys, go to the shop and get me one."

Gladys Darby pinched her lips. "The shops are closed."

Popov turned on her. "Find a pub, then!"

Miss Darby's eyes narrowed in a manner that made it clear she didn't like being bossed about, yet she spun on her heel anyway to do Popov's bidding.

Ginger's throat felt as if it were closing up. She tried to push the image of the cold drink out of her mind and managed to choke out, "Why did you kill them?"

"Since you're going to die soon anyway, I'll tell you. Your Lord Whitmore was losing his marbles, as they say in America, and I couldn't risk him giving away to your people any Russian secrets he might've learned along the way. As for Fedorov—Milestone—he was getting sloppy."

Ginger shook her head at the man's blatant disregard for human life. His willingness to commit murder for minor offences, indeed his desire to kill at all, caused Ginger to shiver. Her neck pulsed with fear. She was face to face with a heartless killer.

They both straightened when the sound of the front door creaked open, and male voices floated in.

"It's unlocked, sir?"

"How odd."

Ginger's heart stopped. *Basil and Constable Braxton!* But before she could call out, Maxim Popov slammed his rough hand over her mouth. "Quiet, or they die."

Ginger held in the groan she felt building in her gut. *Leave, leave, leave.* If only Basil and Constable Braxton would simply turn around and go back to their cars.

But Miss Darby had left the lights on.

"You're sure the M.M. on the cleaver stands for Mason'sMeats, sir?"

"I'm not sure, but it's a possibility."

Maxim Popov indicated Ginger should stand by poking her ribs with the muzzle of his pistol. He forced her into a corner where they were both concealed by the shadow cast by the shelving unit.

Basil called out, "Hello? Anyone here?"

Ginger's skin prickled as fear bit at her nerves. Maxim Popov's palm tightened against her mouth, smelling of sweat. The man needn't worry about her. Ginger would never do anything that would put Basil's life at risk.

Constable Braxton's voice carried along the high ceiling. "Do you think our victim worked here, sir?"

"That, or possibly his killer."

"What do you hope to find, sir?"

"I was hoping to find the owner. Why would he leave without turning out the lights or locking the door?"

The noise of feet shuffling in the butchering area and drawers squeaking open and closed seemed to echo around the room.

"I don't see anyone here, sir."

"Is there a room at the back?"

Ginger held her breath. If they investigated further, they'd find the chairs and evidence of a meeting room. Though the door to the back was concealed to look like a pantry, close inspection would reveal otherwise.

"Just a pantry, sir. Tubs of lard and the like."

"Check the cold storage," Basil said.

"Yes, sir, and then, if it's all right with you, would you mind—"

"Mind what, Constable?"

"Oh, nothing, sir."

"Speak your mind."

"It's just that Miss Gold is waiting for me. So, once we've finished here."

Ginger could picture Basil's mouth, his lips pinching to hold in a smile. Her husband was a tough police officer and a cunning investigator, but she knew him better than most. Basil had a soft spot for romance.

"Go on," Basil said. "I'll finish up."

"You're sure, sir?"

"Yes. But don't be late for work tomorrow morning."

"Sir. Thank you, sir."

Ginger held her breath. Basil only needed to leave with Constable Braxton, and all would be well. The main door slammed closed. Ginger strained to hear footsteps—had Basil gone too?

A harsh silence filled the space. Maxim Popov slowly released his hold on Ginger's mouth, and she let out a long breath. She was still a captive, but at least Basil and Constable Braxton were safe.

Popov pushed her back to the chair, and she fell onto it with a *thunk*.

Ginger braced herself for the continuance of the interrogation, but then the worst thing she could imagine happened.

The movable pantry door shifted open, and Basil stepped into the room.

"*A*hh," Popov began, "the good Chief Inspector Reed has decided to join us."

Ginger locked eyes with Basil, whose hazel eyes darkened in horror.

"Ginger?"

"I'm sorry, Basil."

Popov clicked his tongue, his pistol pointing at Basil's chest. "A romantic reunion." He turned the gun on Ginger. "Hands behind your back, mister."

Miss Darby chose that moment to return with the glass bottle of soda in her hand. Popov snatched the drink and demanded, "Tie them."

If Miss Darby was surprised to see Basil in the room, she kept it to herself and moved quickly to do as commanded.

Ginger had no doubt that the task of tying Basil's

wrists was well done. Her own burning wrists were a testament to that.

"What's going on?" Basil said. "I know Miss Darby, but who are you?"

"You don't know?" Popov looked at Ginger and made a tutting sound. "Are you keeping secrets from your husband too?"

Basil narrowed his eyes at Ginger.

"This man killed Lord Whitmore," Ginger said.

Basil shot Popov a scathing glare. "Did you kill Frederick Milestone as well?" He glanced at Ginger. "Is that why the cleaver that killed him came from here?"

Ginger didn't know the answer and cast her gaze back to their captor.

"You are rather naive, Chief Inspector." Popov's lips lifted into that annoying crooked smile. "His name wasn't Milestone." His eyes darkened as if he'd just had an evil idea. Shifting a wooden ladder-back chair behind Ginger, he commanded Basil. "Take a seat. Please."

Basil focused on Ginger, the questions in his eyes pulsing, until he was forced to turn away. He lowered himself into the chair Popov had placed against hers. Ginger shivered at Basil's nearness, the warmth of his back next to hers.

Popov instructed Miss Darby further. "Bind them together."

Basil pressed on. "If his name wasn't Milestone, then what was it?"

"We knew him in Russia as Pavel Fedorov."

"Russia," Basil spat. "You're a member of the Communist Party?"

Popov cackled, then dropped his English accent, letting the sounds of his native land bleed through. "Mrs. Reed, do you not confide in your husband at all?"

"Ginger?" Basil's voice was tight. "What is he talking about?"

Instead of answering, Ginger stared hard at Popov. "What are you going to do with us?" she asked.

Popov chuckled. "Just a bit of fun." He opened the door of a worn-looking cabinet and removed a box. "Ah, I thought there was one left."

Ginger stiffened as Popov removed an item and presented it as though it were a delicate gift. A *bomb*.

Miss Darby blanched. "Do you need me to stay?"

Popov shrugged. "You may go. Put out the word that there will be an emergency meeting tomorrow." He sniggered. "A new location will be announced."

"Who *are* you?" Basil's voice was strained, and Ginger didn't miss the fear laced in it.

"You can call me Mr. Ironside."

Ginger felt she owed Basil some explanation. "His name is Maxim Popov. He's a Soviet spy."

"And you know this how?"

Ginger glared at Popov. He sneered in return. "You might as well tell him the truth, Mrs. Reed."

"Ginger?" Basil pleaded. "Tell me what you know."

"I'll tell you what *I* know," Popov said. "I know that you don't know your wife at all."

"That's enough," Ginger said. She sighed. Basil deserved the truth if he would die because of her.

"Basil, love. You know I worked in France during the war."

"Yes, as a telephone operator."

"Yes, but not only that."

"What do you mean?"

Even now, with the threat of dying, Ginger couldn't bring herself to break her oath. She swallowed hard. "All I can say is that there are things that happened during the war that I'm not allowed to tell anyone. I hope you can understand."

Her husband wasn't stupid. Everyone knew about the secret service. People just didn't know who worked for them.

Ginger felt Basil's shoulders slump. He responded quietly, "So many things make sense now."

"I wish I could give you lovebirds more time to

get acquainted," Popov said, "but I'd really like to get on with things." He patted his stomach. "I am hungry."

While Ginger had been confessing, Popov had rigged the bomb. He had run a long wire from the spindle knob on Ginger's chair to a pin jutting out of the contraption which sat precariously on the table.

"See," he said facetiously. "I'm not a monster. I'm giving you time to catch up on all your lies. So long as you don't move, you'll be fine. Try to get away, you'll pull the bomb off the table, and everything will go *boom*." His fists burst open as if to demonstrate the effect. "This little beauty is on a timer, so either way, you've only got—you know, I'm going to keep that a *secret*."

Then, as if to explain why he didn't just shoot them, he unlocked the hammer of his pistol. "No bullets."

Ginger closed her eyes, defeated. All this time, Popov's pistol hadn't even been loaded. Just before Popov disappeared through the pantry door, he smiled again. "*Proshchay*. Farewell."

The sound of their shallow breathing and the soft ticking of the bomb felt like it played on a gramophone, loud, filling the room. Ginger's mind raced. There had to be a way to beat this. If they shifted their chairs to the table, they might release the pin. Even if they got there, what could they do with their hands tied between the chair backs?

Ginger felt Basil rubbing the rope around his wrists against the edge of one of the supporting boards on the back of his chair. She whispered, "Be careful."

Ginger scoured the room. There had to be something they could use to free themselves.

Basil paused, then broke the silence. "How did you get involved with Popov? Who approached you?"

Ginger sighed with regret. There was no point in keeping information that Basil wanted from him if they were only going to die in a few minutes. "Captain Smithwick."

"*Smithwick?*"

Basil and Captain Smithwick were acquainted, and bad blood ran between them.

"We . . . er . . . met in France."

"Did Daniel know?"

Ginger heard the question behind the question. Had her first husband known of this other life when her current husband had not?

"No, he didn't." She'd kept her secret from Daniel and was convinced her lack of honesty had contributed to his death during the war. She had been in possession of information that, had Daniel known the same, he could've made a life-saving manoeuvre, not only preserving himself but the soldiers with him.

Now she would be responsible for Basil's death too.

She blamed Captain Smithwick. He'd warned her to keep her vow of secrecy, and she'd lost sleep over how she'd been deceiving Basil. If she'd told him what she knew, if she'd broken the oath, they might've solved the case together, found Lord Whitmore's murderer, and shut down the communist cell.

Ginger's stomach clenched with fear. Not of dying, but of losing Basil just before dying.

"Basil, love, I'm truly sorry."

"Please, don't apologise. We can't give up! Ginger, I'm not ready for this, for us, to end."

How could they be in such a difficult situation? If they moved, they would die, if they didn't, they would die. What they needed was a miracle. Ginger looked heavenward, a silent prayer on her lips.

And then the door crashed open.

## 23

The intruder stopped in his tracks. Even in silhouette, Ginger knew the man.

"Captain Smithwick?"

"I got your note."

He took a step, and Ginger shook her head. "No. Stop. If you trip on that wire, the place will explode."

Quick to calculate the situation, Captain Smithwick eased to the table and studied the bomb.

"Three minutes, forty-one seconds."

Ginger couldn't stop the wave of panic. "Hurry. Untie us!"

Captain Smithwick reached into his boot, produced a Swiss army knife, and cut through Ginger's binding. "Hello, Chief Inspector. I'm sure you have a lot of questions."

Ginger, now free, sprang to her feet. "Just hurry."

She rubbed her wrists, which burned as the circulation returned.

Desperation filled Basil's eyes. "Go!"

She hesitated, not wanting to leave without Basil, but Captain Smithwick had done quick work, and Basil was suddenly at her side grabbing her hand. As they raced to the door, Ginger glanced over her shoulder at Captain Smithwick.

"Are you coming?"

"I know these kinds of bombs. I can defuse it."

"Francis!" Ginger never used the captain's first name, but the urgency demanded it. "Leave it be!"

Captain Smithwick was already at work, head bent low over the apparatus. "If it blows, the whole street will go. Innocent lives may be lost. I can manage it, Ginger. Go!"

Basil wasn't in the mood to argue with the man and tugged on Ginger's hand. "Come on. I'm sure he knows what he's doing."

Ginger didn't think Basil was that sure. He had them running down the corridor as fast as they could go, Ginger hopping behind on one shoe, and didn't stop until they were a safe distance across the street and down the lane. The night was pitch black, but a gas street lamp on the corner shed a dim light. Flashing his police identification with authority, Basil warned the few pedestrians to stay back and take another route. A foot officer jogged over.

"What's the meaning of this?" Then, on recognising Basil said, "Sorry, sir. Might I help, sir?"

"Hurry to a police box and call for help. Tell them to send a bomb expert to this address."

The officer flinched. "A bomb, sir?"

Basil pointed. "Go now!"

"Yes, sir!" The officer raced away. Ginger didn't know how a bomb expert could help. There was no way one could get there and defuse the bomb before the timer went off.

It was up to Captain Smithwick.

Ginger's eyes stayed on the door of the butcher's shop. How much time had passed? Perhaps Captain Smithwick had succeeded? She watched with expectation, waiting for the captain to stroll out onto the street any second with that smug look she despised plastered on his face.

She might even forgive him now. She'd have to, rather, since he'd just saved both her own and Basil's lives.

*Come on, Captain!*

Then, the earth shook. The boom Maxim Popov had predicted happened, throwing Ginger to the ground.

inger loved the end-of-the-day routine she and Basil had settled into since their marriage and the subsequent adoption of Scout. After a delicious dinner prepared by Mrs. Beasley, Scout would take Boss out for his evening constitutional as Ginger and Basil enjoyed a glass of brandy in front of the fireplace in the sitting room. She relished how they shared the events of their days. Though their cases occasionally intersected, most days their news was fresh to the ears of the other.

Other members of the family joined in occasionally, and Ambrosia and Felicia now occupied the armchairs whilst sipping sherry, and Scout taught Boss to roll over. Of course, Boss already knew the trick, but the terrier loved the game.

And though they no longer needed coal to keep the house toasty—the weather had suddenly turned unseasonably warm—a full bucket sat on the hearth. The mermaid, from her perch above the mantel, seemed to wink at Ginger. Ginger had a secret, and she'd whispered it earlier to the mythical creature in the painting, just to hear what it sounded like spoken aloud.

That evening, all the family had gathered. Felicia, radiantly youthful, her bow lips tinted red by the sherry, looked a little put out. She was without a date that evening after admitting to Ginger she wasn't ready to commit to either Constable Braxton or Mr. Fulton, and frowned in Ginger's direction as if her lack of male companionship was somehow Ginger's fault.

Ambrosia seemed somewhat aware of Felicia's predicament, and her cheeks rounded in a smile as she prepared to make an announcement.

"I've invited Mr. Algernon Longstaff to dinner."

*Oh mercy*, Ginger thought. Ambrosia was up to her old tricks. Poor Felicia.

Felicia protested, "Grandmama! Not on my account, I hope."

"I'm not asking you to marry the gentleman, only to be polite. Besides, he's from a good family. His cousin is the Earl of Hadston, and he's recently inherited a goodly sum. And even better, he's of an age where a man is generally looking for a wife."

Felicia moaned into her sherry glass.

Beseeching her support, Ambrosia stared across the room at Ginger. "Surely, you must side with me, Georgia. Felicia is nearly *twenty-four*. She'll soon be regarded as a spinster!"

Basil hid a smile behind his brandy glass and shot Ginger a sympathetic sideways glance. Ginger hated being pulled into the middle of this tiresome argument between grandmother and granddaughter.

Felicia came to her own defence. "I'm not going to die a spinster, Grandmama. There are plenty of eligible men who'd get on their knee with the slightest encouragement. I'm just not ready yet."

Ambrosia couldn't hold in her exasperation. "What on earth are you waiting for?"

"Love," Felicia shot back. "I'm waiting to fall in love." Her gaze latched on to Ginger. "I want to be in love with someone the way Ginger and Basil are in love. Is that so much to ask?"

Ambrosia worked her wrinkled lips. Ginger couldn't very well crush Felicia by saying that love like she and Basil shared didn't come around to everyone. How could she, when it had come for her twice already?

"Felicia, love," Ginger started, feeling like she had to say something. "You'll meet someone and fall in love, I'm sure, but don't expect love at first sight." She squeezed Basil's hand. "Deep love is something you grow into."

Felicia huffed. "I suppose I have to eat dinner somewhere tomorrow anyway, but Grandmama, please, please, stop inviting men over for dinner in hopes of finding me a husband."

"How will you manage to find one then?"

"I don't know. But it won't be like that."

Ginger couldn't help but feel sorry for Felicia and wasn't surprised when her sister-in-law finished her sherry and announced that she was going to bed. Ambrosia left soon afterwards.

"Why does Grandmother Ambrosia want Aunt Felicia to get married so badly?"

So caught up in Felicia and Ambrosia's standoff, Ginger had almost forgotten about Scout being in the room.

"I don't understand why anyone has to get married," Scout continued, a look of disgust on his young face.

Ginger glanced sideways at Basil, who thankfully stepped in.

"Matters of the heart are one of life's mysteries, Scout," he said. "Keep Boss as close as you can. He'll be your best chum over the next few years."

Ginger grinned. Before long, Scout was bound to

notice the gentler sex and then how life in Hartigan House would change!

Yes, significant changes were coming to the house.

"Scout," Ginger started. "Time for bed."

Scout appeared disheartened at the prospect of bedtime, but Boss whined as his stubby tail dusted the floor as he stared up at Scout with round, playful eyes.

"All right, old boy, let's go."

Ginger laughed as she watched the two skip out of the room. Life was good. As she snuggled next to Basil, she began to muse about the last two weeks. Maxim Popov and Gladys Darby had been captured and arrested for their parts in the murders of Lord Whitmore and Frederick Milestone/Pavel Fedorov and for the attempted murder of Basil and herself. It was revealed that Miss Darby had been an orphan who'd done whatever she had to to survive the hard streets of London, and Ginger felt a tremendous amount of sympathy for her, despite her horrible misdeeds. Maxim Popov had offered her a lifeline of sorts, one made of thread.

The miners' lockout ended, to the disappointment of many, without concession to the miners, who in many ways had ended up worse off. As Captain Smithwick—may he rest in peace—had predicted, many joined the Communist Party of Great Britain. Ginger feared the battle for communism would be extended. Harold Bronson admitted to being enticed by the message, but hadn't, like many miners who'd returned to work, joined the party. Ginger had encouraged Harold and Angela to stay on, but Angela missed her family who resided in Durham.

Captain Smithwick's act of heroism—or was it egotism—had ultimately saved Ginger and Basil's lives, and for that Ginger would be eternally grateful. Though she still held the captain responsible for Daniel's death, her heart had softened with something very close to forgiveness. She and Basil had attended his funeral to honour him and say goodbye. For Ginger, it was a dramatic ending to a chapter of her life now best put to rest.

It turned out that Leo Tipper had been romantically involved with Miss Darby but thought he was onto a story about sexual scandal amongst the Lords and had no idea of the real story under his nose. Ginger, after getting the all-clear from Scotland Yard, had called Blake Brown as she'd promised and told him everything she was permitted to say about the turn of events. Lord Whitmore was well known in London and his death couldn't go unremarked, however, she'd withheld certain unpleasant details.

Ginger set her brandy glass aside and reached for Basil's hand.

"Basil, love, I have something to tell you."

The natural smile on her husband's handsome face faded. He and Ginger never spoke of her reluctant disclosure about her wartime activities, and Basil, thankfully, had never pressed her on it except for one night, shortly after Captain Smithwick had died, when he'd asked about her first husband.

"How did Daniel die?"

The question had been a spear to her heart. They were getting ready for bed, and Ginger's knees turned to mud as she lowered herself onto the stool of her dressing table. "You know I can't talk about it."

"Please, Ginger, just this one thing, then I promise never to bring up your past again."

Ginger owed Basil this, she knew she did. She compromised by telling the story without mentioning any names.

"As you know, whoever controlled the bridges, directed the war. There was a bridge in France that the Germans had commandeered. It had been well used by the enemy for months and heavily manned. A certain . . . er . . . captain gave orders to a certain brigade to collapse the bridge with whatever means. It was a suicide mission. Everyone knew it, but the captain was too proud to call the brigade back."

"And you?"

"I'd overheard the captain send the orders. I waited

too long to send a warning. By the time it reached the brigade, it was too late. Only one British soldier survived to tell the tale."

It had been a sobering moment, but Basil kept his word and never brought up matters about the Great War again.

"Is everything all right?" he now asked, bringing her back to the moment.

Ginger faced Basil and nibbled on her lip. What she was about to tell him, she could hardly believe herself.

"I visited Dr. Longden."

Basil's hazel eyes flashed with worry. Ginger had been concerned about her overall health. Overly exhausted lately, she often felt as if she were coming down with something.

"I'm expecting a baby."

It was a good thing Basil had sipped the last of his brandy because his empty glass slipped out of his hand and onto the carpet. His lashes blinked as he processed the news.

"But I thought—"

"So did I. But my mother conceived late in life after years of nothing." Ginger stared back, hopeful. "It happens."

She wouldn't think about her mother having died

shortly after Ginger had been born. History didn't have to repeat itself in every way. Deciding not to live in fear, she would be happy for this miracle.

"Basil?"

Basil gently cupped her face with his palms and drew her close. He kissed her deeply, and when he pulled away, his eyes shone with excitement.

"You're happy?" Ginger asked eagerly.

Basil laughed. "I'm delighted!"

Ginger joined in. "Oh, Basil. I can't believe we're going to have a baby!"

---

If you enjoyed reading *Murder on Fleet Street* please help others enjoy it too.

**Recommend it:** Help others find the book by recommending it to friends, readers' groups, discussion boards and by **suggesting it to your local library.**

**Review it:** Please tell other readers why you liked this book by reviewing it on Amazon or Goodreads.

## GENDER REVEAL!

THE SECRET's out ~ Ginger and Basil are having a baby!!

In our modern day and age, we no longer have the patience to wait nine months to find out if the baby is a boy or a girl, and you don't have to wait either.

Ginger and Basil are having a baby girl!

Spring ahead twenty-eight years to 1956, and you can meet Miss Rosa Reed when she eventually opens up her own private detective office in the fictional town of Santa Bonita.

What's a girl, born and bred in London, England, doing in a small town on the Pacific coast of America?

You'll have to read to find out! The first four books in the new Rosa Reed Mystery series is available to preorder now.

## MURDER AT HIGH TIDE
a Rosa Reed Mystery

## Murder's all wet!

It's 1956 and WPC (Woman Police Constable) Rosa Reed has left her groom at the altar in London. Time spent with her American cousins in Santa Bonita, California is exactly what she needs to get back on her feet, though the last thing she expected was to get entangled in another murder case!

If you love early rock & roll, poodle skirts, clever who-dun-its, a charming cat and an even more charming detective, you're going to love this new series!

Buy on Amazon or read Free with Kindle Unlimited!

## MURDER ON THE BOARDWALK
a Rosa Reed Mystery

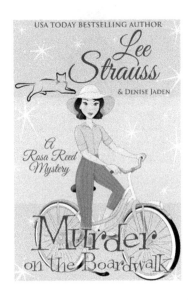

Buy on Amazon or read Free with Kindle Unlimited!

## MURDER AT THE BOMB SHELTER
a Rosa Reed Mystery

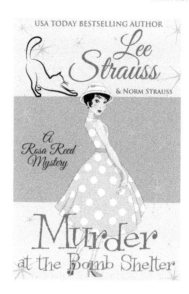

Buy on Amazon or read Free with Kindle Unlimited!

# MURDER ON LOCATION
a Rosa Reed Mystery

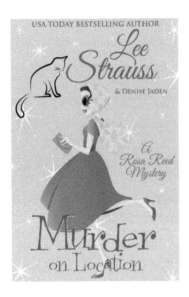

Buy on Amazon or read Free with Kindle Unlimited!

# AFTERWORD

This is where I admit to taking artistic license when it comes to the historical General Strike in May 1926 that brought much of England's trades and transit to a halt for several days. Though there were resulting uprisings and chaos in the streets, to my knowledge, there were never any bombings. That event found in this fictional document is a product of my imagination.

## GINGER GOLD'S JOURNAL

Sign up for Lee's readers list and gain access to **Ginger Gold's private Journal.** Find out about Ginger's Life before the SS *Rosa* and how she became the woman she has. This is a fluid document that will cover her romance with her late husband Daniel, her time serving in the British secret service during World War One, and beyond. Includes a recipe for Dark Dutch Chocolate Cake!

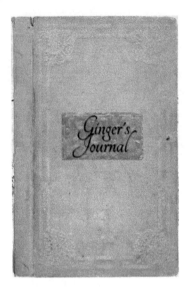

It begins: **July 31, 1912**

How fabulous that I found this Journal today, hidden in the bottom of my wardrobe. Good old Pippins, our English butler in London, gave it to me as a parting gift when Father whisked me away on our American adventure so he could marry Sally. Pips said it was for me to record my new adventures. I'm ashamed I never even penned one word before today. I think I was just too sad.

This old leather-bound journal takes me back to that emotional time. I had shed enough tears to fill the ocean and I remember telling Father dramatically that I was certain to cause flooding to match God's. At eight years old I was well-trained in my biblical studies, though, in retro-spect, I would say that I had probably bordered on heresy with my little tantrum.

The first week of my "adventure" was spent with a tummy ache and a number of embarrassing sessions that involved a bucket and Father holding back my long hair so I wouldn't soil it with vomit.

I certainly felt that I was being punished for some reason. Hartigan House—though large and sometimes lonely—was my home and Pips was my good friend. He often helped me to pass the time with games of I Spy and Xs and Os.

"Very good, Little Miss," he'd say with a twinkle in his blue eyes when I won, which I did often. I suspect now that our good butler wasn't beyond letting me win even when unmerited.

Father had got it into his silly head that I needed a mother, but I think the truth was he wanted a wife. Sally, a woman half my father's age, turned out to be a sufficient wife in the end, but I could never claim her as a mother.

Well, Pips, I'm sure you'd be happy to

know that things turned out all right here in America.

SUBSCRIBE to read more!

.

## MORE FROM LEE STRAUSS

## On AMAZON

## GINGER GOLD MYSTERY SERIES (cozy 1920s historical)

*Cozy. Charming. Filled with Bright Young Things. This Jazz Age murder mystery will entertain and delight you with its 1920s flair and pizzazz!*

Murder on the SS Rosa

Murder at Hartigan House

Murder at Bray Manor

Murder at Feathers & Flair

Murder at the Mortuary

Murder at Kensington Gardens

Murder at St. George's Church

The Wedding of Ginger & Basil

Murder Aboard the Flying Scotsman

Murder at the Boat Club

Murder on Eaton Square

Murder by Plum Pudding

Murder on Fleet Street

**LADY GOLD INVESTIGATES (Ginger Gold companion short stories)**

Volume 1

Volume 2

Volume 3

**HIGGINS & HAWKE MYSTERY SERIES (cozy 1930s historical)**

*The 1930s meets Rizzoli & Isles in this friendship depression era cozy mystery series.*

Death at the Tavern

Death on the Tower

Death on Hanover

THE ROSA REED MYSTERIES

(1950s cozy historical)

Murder at High Tide

Murder on the Boardwalk

Murder at the Bomb Shelter

Murder on Location

**A NURSERY RHYME MYSTERY SERIES(mystery/sci fi)**

*Marlow finds himself teamed up with intelligent and savvy Sage Farrell, a girl so far out of his league he feels blinded in her presence - literally - damned glasses! Together they work to find the identity of @gingerbreadman. Can they stop the killer before he strikes again?*

Gingerbread Man

Life Is but a Dream

Hickory Dickory Dock

Twinkle Little Star

## THE PERCEPTION TRILOGY (YA dystopian mystery)

*Zoe Vanderveen is a GAP—a genetically altered person. She lives in the security of a walled city on prime water-front property along side other equally beautiful people with extended life spans. Her brother Liam is missing. Noah Brody, a boy on the outside, is the only one who can help ~ but can she trust him?*

Perception

Volition

Contrition

## LIGHT & LOVE (sweet romance)

*Set in the dazzling charm of Europe, follow Katja, Gabriella, Eva, Anna and Belle as they find strength, hope and love.*

Sing me a Love Song

Your Love is Sweet

In Light of Us

Lying in Starlight

## PLAYING WITH MATCHES (WW2 history/romance)

*A sobering but hopeful journey about how one young German boy copes with the war and propaganda. Based on true events.*

A Piece of Blue String (companion short story)

THE CLOCKWISE COLLECTION (YA time travel romance)

*Casey Donovan has issues: hair, height and uncontrollable trips to the 19th century! And now this ~ she's accidentally taken Nate Mackenzie, the cutest boy in the school, back in time. Awkward.*

Clockwise

Clockwiser

Like Clockwork

Counter Clockwise

Clockwork Crazy

Clocked (companion novella)

Standalones

**As Elle Lee Strauss**

Seaweed

Love, Tink

Lee Strauss is a USA TODAY bestselling author of The Ginger Gold Mysteries series, The Higgins & Hawke Mystery series, The Rosa Reed Mystery series (cozy historical mysteries), A Nursery Rhyme Mystery series (mystery suspense), The Perception series (young adult dystopian), The Light & Love series (sweet romance), The Clockwise Collection (YA time travel romance), and young adult historical fiction with over a million books read. She has titles published in German, Spanish and Korean, and a growing audio library.

When Lee's not writing or reading she likes to cycle, hike, and play pickleball. She loves to drink caffè lattes and red wines in exotic places, and eat dark chocolate anywhere.

For more info on books by Lee Strauss and her social media links, visit leestraussbooks.com. To make sure you don't miss the next new release, be sure to sign up for her readers' list!

Did you know you can follow your favourite authors on Bookbub? If you subscribe to Bookbub — (and if you don't, why don't you? - They'll send you daily emails alerting you to sales and new releases on just the kind of books you like to read!) — follow me to make sure you don't miss the next Ginger Gold Mystery!

www.leestraussbooks.com
leestraussbooks@gmail.com